PU

WOLF

Mysterious footsteps come padding through the darkness to Nan's flat, and Cassy, awake in the middle of the night, hears voices and someone arriving. The next morning Nan packs her off to stay with Goldie, her beautiful, childish mother.

There is no explanation. But it has all happened before and Cassy knows it is pointless to ask questions. And in any case, she is soon roped into the theatre show called *Wolf* which Goldie, her friend Lyall and his son Robert are rehearsing.

But this distraction is not enough. Something has gone frighteningly wrong and danger is coming after Cassy. The questions mount up, until she can't ignore them any more.

And behind them all lurks the dark wolf-shape which seems to slink into everything.

Even her dreams.

Gillian Cross worked in a school and a bakery before studying at Oxford and Sussex universities. She has also been a child-minder and an assistant to an MP. She has been writing children's books for more than ten years. Her titles in Puffin include *The Demon Headmaster*, *The Prime Minister's Brain* and *On the Edge*. Her hobbies are orienteering and playing the piano.

WOLF

GILLIAN CROSS

PUFFIN BOOKS

PUFFIN BOOKS

Published by the Penguin Group
Penguin Books Ltd, 27 Wrights Lane, London W8 5TZ, England
Penguin Books USA Inc., 375 Hudson Street, New York, New York 10014, USA
Penguin Books Australia Ltd, Ringwood, Victoria, Australia
Penguin Books Canada Ltd, 10 Alcorn Avenue, Toronto, Ontario, Canada M4V 3B2
Penguin Books (NZ) Ltd, 182–190 Wairau Road, Auckland 10, New Zealand

Penguin Books Ltd, Registered Offices: Harmondsworth, Middlesex, England

First published Oxford University Press 1990
Published in Puffin Books 1992
7 9 10 8

WOLF

Of course Cassy never dreams, Nan always said. *She has more sense, to be sure. Her head touches the pillow and she's off, just like any other sensible person. There's been no trouble with dreams, not since she was a baby.*

CHAPTER 1

He came in the early morning, at about half past two. His feet padded along the balcony, slinking silently past the closed doors of the other flats. No one glimpsed his shadow flickering across the curtain or noticed the uneven rhythm of his steps.

But he woke Cassy. She lay in her bed under the window and listened as the footsteps stopped outside. There were two quick, light taps on the front door. Then a pause and then two more taps, like a signal.

Cassy sat up slowly. She heard the door of the back room open and Nan come hurrying out. Not running (*nurses never run, except for fire or haemorrhage*), but crossing the tiny hall in two quick strides.

The front door handle clicked, but no one spoke and no light from the hall showed under Cassy's door. He came in quickly, in silence, in the dark, and the door closed behind him at once.

He and Nan crept into the back room and for a split second Cassy caught the sound of his voice, but she couldn't make out any words. Then the door swung shut and both voices merged into a steady, muffled drone, matching the drone of traffic that floated into Cassy's other ear, from the West Way.

She lay down again and closed her eyes, wiping her mind clean and willing the questions away. *Mind your own business*, Nan always said, *and you won't get your nose caught in my mousetrap*.

No questions. No thinking at all. The blankness came easily, from long practice, and she floated into a dreamless sleep.

When she woke up again it was morning. Nan was standing at the foot of the bed, beside the chest of drawers. On top of the chest, level with Nan's face, was the big, framed photograph of

3

Cassy's father as a little boy. Both of them stood very straight, shining clean, but not smiling. Mother and son.

Nan was staring straight at Cassy, but the boy's eyes were gazing into the distance, fixed on something beyond the picture. For a second, floating up out of sleep, Cassy wondered what it was.

Then she saw the old brown suitcase in Nan's right hand.

She sat up and frowned, trying to ignore it. 'Why are you still here? I thought you had an early.'

'I was sick,' Nan said. She looked Cassy straight in the eye. 'In the night. They don't want me at work like that.'

Cassy looked straight back, still avoiding the suitcase. 'I'll go and phone Sister for you.'

'No need,' said Nan. 'I'll get Mrs Ramage to phone later on. There's other things for you to do.' She knelt down, laying the suitcase flat on the floor in front of the chest of drawers. 'You'll be better off at your mother's, until I'm over this.'

'Oh, Nan!'

Don't you want me to stay and look after you? Cassy was supposed to say that next. Then Nan would smile and shake her head, lifting the neat piles of clothes into the case. Step by step, word by word, they would go through the same pattern as last time—and all the times before. And at the end of the pattern Cassy would be leaning out of Goldie's window, waving goodbye to Nan. With the brown suitcase lying on the floor behind her.

When she was three—or four?—she had jumped on to the suitcase and banged on the window with her fists. 'Don't leave me here! I want to go with you, Nan!' Even now, the memory brought a ghost of that panic. The miserable terror she had felt as she stood at the window, with Goldie trying to cuddle her, while Nan disappeared round the corner. She never shouted like that again. Better to wave and smile, and pretend it was all right.

But why did it have to happen?

'Why *now*?' The words burst out, even though Nan frowned at her. 'We have to choose our options tomorrow, and I'll never get what I want if I'm not there. Why have I got to go *now*?'

'You don't need a reason to visit your own mother,' Nan said

4

sharply. She opened the catches of the case with a hard, metallic click. 'It must be six months since you saw her.'

'But my options are *important*. You said they were. You said I had to choose very, very carefully.'

'That's as may be,' Nan said. Her voice was cold, and she didn't look at Cassy. 'But there's more to life than school. Now get up and get yourself washed.'

Briskly she opened the first drawer and began to take out Cassy's clothes. Three vests, worn thin but washed white. Six pairs of knickers. Two good jumpers and one with a darned elbow.

But Cassy wasn't ready to give up yet. She stared stubbornly down at the half-packed suitcase.

'I want to know what this is all for. *Why* have I got to go so suddenly?'

'There's no time to spare for chattering,' Nan said. She folded a navy-blue school skirt into three, precisely, without looking at Cassy. 'Stop asking questions and get yourself washed.'

Cassy pushed her feet into her slippers and padded towards the bedroom door. As she stepped into the hall, she glanced quickly at the door of the back room. It was shut. Of course. She had never said anything to Nan, or tried to work out the connection in her own mind. But she knew that the strangeness of the closed door went with the strangeness of the suitcase.

She couldn't remember when she had first noticed, but it was always like that. Usually, Nan insisted on keeping the back room door open, to air the room. It was her bedroom as well as the sitting room, and she hated it to smell of sleep. Even though it faced the front door, it was always wide open.

Except when the brown suitcase appeared. Then, suddenly, the back room door would be closed and Cassy knew that she must leave it alone. The only time that Nan had ever smacked her was when she had touched the handle once, to see what would happen.

Today, because she was angry, she stood and stared at it. The back of her neck tingled. She wanted to march across to that door and fling it wide open, to let in the fresh air.

But, out of the corner of her eye, she could see Nan

watching her. She was sitting back on her heels with her hands in her lap, looking at Cassy with narrowed eyes. Waiting for her to turn away from the back room and go into the bathroom.

Cassy shut the bathroom door tight and glared at her reflection in the mirror. Sensible brown eyes. Sensible short brown hair. You only had to look at that face to know she wouldn't do anything wild. *If everyone was like you*, Nan said, *the world would be a simpler, sweeter place*. Sometimes Cassy wished being sensible wasn't so important.

She washed twice as fast as usual, but even so Nan was calling before she had finished. 'What are you doing in there, child? Your breakfast's ready.'

'Coming.' Cassy folded her towel and hung it on the rail. Then she walked out of the bathroom. 'What shall I do with my pyjamas?'

'Put them in the wash,' Nan said, from the kitchen. 'I've packed some clean ones. Then get dressed and come to have your porridge.'

By the time Cassy walked into the kitchen, her porridge was out and her tea was poured. Before she had even sat down, Nan was pushing the milk and sugar at her and talking about the next thing.

'I've put up a bag of food for you to take. Will you manage that as well as your suitcase?'

Cassy stopped, with a spoonful of sugar in mid air. 'Why have I got to carry them both? Aren't you going to come with me?'

'And why would you need me to hold your hand? You may not be very big, but you're almost fourteen,' Nan turned away quickly and began to run water into the porridge saucepan. 'I don't want to be running around on trains. Not in my state of health.'

'But you *always* take me.'

'Maybe it's time you were growing up, then,' Nan said. But she spoke in a strange, offhand way. She was thinking of something else.

Cassy sprinkled the sugar and poured the milk. The porridge stuck in her throat like cotton wool, but she ate it just the same, watching Nan unzip her battered old purse and count out the train fare on to the table.

As the last ten pence went on the top of the pile, Nan hesitated for a moment, her fingers hovering. Then she pulled out a crumpled note and laid it down beside the coins.

'You can take that, too. Just in case. But don't spend it unless you have to. And don't let your mother know that you've got it.'

Twenty pounds? But that was a huge amount of money. Cassy put her spoon down and stared at it. Nan had never given her that much before.

'Why on earth—?'

But there was no chance to ask. Nan went straight on talking, in her briskest voice. 'Put it away now, before you lose it.' She pushed the money across the table to Cassy. 'And there's a letter for your mother, too.'

The envelope was sealed and Nan had written *Goldie* on the outside in her small, cramped writing. Cassy picked it up and zipped it into the pocket of her skirt, with the money. As she tucked the twenty-pound note away, she took a deep breath, and spoke very fast, before Nan could interrupt.

'I am coming back? Aren't I?'

For one terrifying second, Nan hesitated. Cassy grabbed the edge of the table and gripped it hard.

'I haven't got to go and live with her for ever?'

'Don't talk nonsense!' Nan snapped. 'You live here, with me. Always have, and always will. You're just going to your mother's until—until I'm better.'

'But can't you say how long it's going to be?'

'I'll write. And you must write to me.'

Nan stood up and went to the drawer by the window where she kept her bits and pieces. She found a packet of plain white postcards and counted out twelve stamps to go with them.

'There you are. I want to hear from you twice a week, now. No need to write an essay, just a note about how you're going on. And keep writing, mind, even if—if I've got no time to write back.'

Cassy took the postcards and turned them over in her hand. They were comforting, in a way, because they meant that Nan wanted to hear from her. But there were a lot of them. Twelve. If she used two a week, they would last her for six weeks. She couldn't imagine what it would be like to live with Goldie for six weeks.

'I'll put them in my case,' she said.

'That's right,' Nan nodded. 'Best to get going now. No point in hanging about when you've a journey to make.'

Moving was better than thinking. Cassy stood up, holding the postcards and the stamps, and walked out into the hall. She did not even glance at the closed door of the back room. It was none of her business. All she had to do was finish packing.

When she flicked the suitcase open, the heaps of clothes looked back bleakly at her. Plain, practical clothes, well cared for, but wearing a little thin. Sensible, unobtrusive things that would never stand out in a crowd.

As she laid the postcards on top, she realized that she had nothing to write with. It was no use relying on Goldie to have a pen, so she turned to take her school pencil-case, from the top of the chest of drawers.

It was lying next to the picture, and the solemn little boy caught Cassy's eye. She picked up the photograph and tilted it to the light, wondering, for the thousandth time, where he was now. Were his eyes still fixed on something that no one else could see? What did he look like?

Mick Phelan.

She shaped the words with her lips, making no sound. Knowing, as she had always known, that they must not be spoken out loud.

'Cassy!' Nan called from the kitchen. 'What are you at? It's time you were on your way.'

Guiltily, Cassy grabbed the pencil-case and, barely realizing what she was doing, crammed photograph and pencil-case, both together, in on top of the postcards. Then she slammed the top and flicked the catches shut.

'Just coming!'

She put on her school mac, pulling the belt tight, and carried the suitcase out into the hall. Nan was waiting by the front door, with the old shopping bag in her hand. She held it out.

'There's a few bits of food for you. Goldie won't have anything in, if I know her, and you'll need a square meal tonight.'

Cassy took the bag. 'What have you put in here? It weighs a ton.'

'It's good solid food for a growing girl,' Nan said. There were two bright pink patches on her cheeks and she was talking faster than usual. 'Now you take good care of it, mind. Don't you go handing it over to Goldie. Keep it all in a good, safe place. Be sure—'

But she did not go on. Instead, she put a firm hand in the middle of Cassy's back and pushed her gently towards the door. 'Don't dally around now. Go straight there. You must know the way well enough.'

'Oh yes. I take the Tube to—'

'Well, there's no need to spell it all out.'

Cassy blinked at the sharp edge to the words. Then she leaned forward to kiss Nan's rough, squashy cheek. 'Don't worry about me. I'll be sensible. And if she's moved, I'll track her down. Bye.'

'You're a good girl.' Nan laid the back of her hand softly against Cassy's cheek. 'Be patient,' she said in a low voice. 'Things will work out.'

The gentleness startled Cassy into silence. Before she could work out what it meant, Nan had taken her hand away, stepped back inside and shut the door.

For a second Cassy stood staring at it, but all she could see was her own reflection in the little glass pane. There was no point in waiting.

She had more sense than to knock on the door again. A couple of years ago, she had quarrelled with Goldie and run away home. When Nan saw her standing on the doorstep, she had sent her straight back, even though it was getting dark. Without a meal or a cup of tea to warm her up. Without even letting her through the front door.

Pulling up the hood of her school mac, Cassy buttoned it firmly under her chin. Then she picked up the heavy suitcase and the shopping bag and set off, a short, determined figure with her head held high.

CHAPTER 2

It took her all day to find Goldie. When she knocked on the door of the bedsit in Notting Hill, a strange woman opened the door. *Bother*, thought Cassy. But it wasn't the first time Goldie had moved without telling them and she knew what to say. She had heard Nan say it often enough, to other strangers.

'I'm very sorry to bother you, but I'm looking for Susan Phelan. Did she leave an address with anyone?'

The woman frowned. 'Dunno. You could try the old guy in the newsagent's. Can't think of anyone else.'

That meant lugging the suitcase and the bag down the road and round the corner, but it was worth it. The man in the newsagent's had a crumpled piece of paper under the counter. He didn't hand it over easily, of course. They never did.

'Daughter?' he said, suspiciously. 'There wasn't no daughter. She lived in that room all on her own.'

'I live with my nan,' said Cassy. 'At least—'

The man looked at her case and chuckled. 'Been evicted? That's what happened to Goldie, too. Rent arrears.'

'And where did she go? Please?'

'We-ell—' The old man looked hard at her and then held out the piece of paper. 'I suppose it's OK. She went off with that boyfriend of hers.'

'Boyfriend?'

'Black man from a squat over in Clapham. She said they worked together.'

Cassy couldn't imagine Goldie working, but she smiled politely, put the piece of paper in her pocket and headed back to the Tube station.

The squat in Clapham had been knocked down, but the people across the road had another address, in Wandsworth.

The squatters in Wandsworth were very helpful indeed. They gave Cassy three cups of tea and an iced bun and asked her lots of questions. Then they told her how to get to the squat in Lambeth where Goldie had gone. ('She helped Lyall and Robert set it up,' said the man called Earl, grinning at the joke.)

By the time she walked out of Lambeth North Tube station, Cassy was exhausted. She had been bumped on the escalators, sworn at as people pushed past her case and followed by an old man with a dirty beret. She was cold and hungry and thirsty and it was getting dark.

But she kept walking. The sides of her hood, like blinkers, shut out the view on either side and her feet moved steadily, with a rhythm of their own. She was beginning to feel that she would never find Goldie. She would just go on and on travelling, from one dingy place to another, until her money was all spent.

By the time she reached Albert Street, the darkness and the hunger and the endless walking had made her light-headed. When she turned the corner, the road ahead of her looked unreal, as if the tall shabby houses were painted on cardboard. She plodded past them, without thinking about the boarded-up windows and the tangled gardens full of rubbish.

Number Forty-Four looked worse than the rest of the row. The boards had been taken down from its bay window and the space behind was very dark. The side alley that led through to the back garden was even darker, and clumps of withered plants straggled against the front wall. Everything was grey or black or dull, shrivelled brown.

Except for two patches of startling colour.

The first was parked outside the house. It was an ordinary Ford Transit van, but it was painted with wild, rainbow shapes. Two elaborate trees twisted up the back doors, climbed round the windows and overflowed on to the roof in an intricate pattern of twigs tangled with stars.

Striding across the side of the van was a pair of vast, giant legs that towered upwards to lose themselves in the stars. Their feet were enormous, but above the ankles they narrowed quickly, stretching up and up, unbelievably tall, until they disappeared into the tree branches on the roof.

Across the legs arched a single word, painted in bold black letters:

MOONGAZER

Cassy stared at it for a second. Then she walked up the front path of the house, towards the other patch of colour.

It was a large notice, stuck up beside the front door. Someone had painted a lively border of flames and weapons and monsters round the edge, but the writing in the middle— carefully protected by polythene—was in stiff, legal language:

TAKE NOTICE it began

THAT *we live in this house, it is our home and we intend to stay here.*

THAT *at all times there is at least one person in this house.*

THAT *any entry into this house without our permission is a CRIMINAL OFFENCE . . .*

No need to read it all. She had seen squatters' notices often enough before. Nan would have sniffed and pinched her lips together to keep the comments in, but Cassy was too tired to disapprove. She skipped the formal words and let her eyes travel straight to the bottom of the sheet.

Signed Lyall Cornelius
Robert Cornelius
Susan Phelan

The Occupiers

At least she had reached the right place. There was no mistaking Goldie's round, irregular writing, with every letter painfully formed. Cassy put down her case and pressed the bell-push.

Nothing happened. After a moment she pressed it again, listening more carefully, but there was no ringing inside the house. The knocker had gone too, and someone had nailed a piece of wood across the letterbox.

In the end, she hammered on the door with the flat of her hand. The thuds were hollow and dead and it was hard to believe there were people inside to hear them. But when she stopped banging she heard the noise of feet running down bare, wooden stairs.

The steps changed, slapping on to tiles, and came right up to the front door. But the door didn't open. Instead, someone spoke from the other side.

'Who is it?'

It was a boy's voice, deep but ragged. Cassy straightened her hood and picked up her suitcase.

'I'm looking for Goldie—for Susan Phelan. Is she there?'

'Who are you?' The question was impersonal. *As though he's filling in a form*, thought Cassy. But that didn't irritate her. It was easier to be business-like.

'I'm her daughter. Cathleen Phelan.'

'Wait a minute.'

He marched down the hall and up the stairs, leaving Cassy to shiver in the dark garden. It smelt of damp earth and rotting leaves, as if she had strayed out of London into a wilder place. When a lighted bus rumbled across the top of Albert Street, it seemed to be moving in another world.

The feet came back. Two heavy bolts slid open, one above Cassy's head and the other level with her feet. Then the hinges creaked as the door swung backwards into the shadows.

The boy was older than she had expected—fifteen or sixteen—and it was hard to make out his face in the darkness. He stepped out of the way politely as Cassy walked into the chilly hall.

'Goldie's up there.' He waved his hand at the stairs. 'Go on up. Don't bother to wait for me.' Shutting the door, he began to tug the bolts back into place.

Cassy walked slowly down the hall, still carrying her suitcase and the bag. It was too dark to see much, but the house had the cave-like smell of mould. The tiles felt broken and uneven under her feet and when she touched the wall loose plaster crumbled away from her fingers.

All her life she had been coming to visit Goldie in places like this. Places with greasy floors and cobwebby ceilings, where smells hung on the stairs and the corners were clogged with dirt. But she had always come with Nan before. And with Nan's scouring powder and scrubbing brush and disinfectant, ready to clean everything up. This time it was different.

13

She climbed the stairs, plodding heavily from step to step, heading for the light that shone, very faintly, on to the landing. It was coming from the room on her right, at the back of the house. Heaving her case another couple of feet, Cassy tapped lightly on the door.

'Come in!'

That was Goldie's voice, giggly and excited. Cassy pushed the door open, took one step—and stopped in confusion.

It was like walking into an infinite forest, full of fireflies.

The darkness flickered with points of flame that dipped and swelled all round her, retreating endlessly. Between the flames were dark flowers and flashes of colour that defied her eyes and teased her mind. Were they large or small? Near or far?

The room had no limits. Left and right, behind and in front and above, the lights and the flowers surrounded her with patterns that destroyed her sense of space. The shock of it froze her brain and she gripped the handle of her suitcase, standing completely still as she worked out where the boundaries were.

It took her more than a minute. Slowly she realized that she was looking at reflections. The only real lights were two candles, standing in bottles in the middle of the floor. Their flames were reflected backwards and forwards, over and over, up and down, in a hundred fragments of mirror.

There were pieces of mirror stuck all over the walls and the ceiling. Some were coloured, some were engraved or bevelled or painted and some were plain. Some were stuck flat to the wall and some were set at an angle. In every piece, the flames danced differently.

Dozens of pieces of cloth were draped round the mirrors, hiding the sharp straight edges and filling the gaps with shadowed images. Sombre flowers were overlapped by plain, dark cloth, and dim leaves twined in and out of dusty velvet. Here and there a few silver folds gleamed white, like silver birch trunks in a wood of yew and holly.

Behind the flames, between the tree trunks, among the shadows, there were human shapes, infinitely reflected and repeated like the candles. But, like the candles, only two of them were real. Slowly Cassy turned to face them.

Goldie was sitting on a mattress in one corner, as still and upright as a doll in a glass case. A black, fringed shawl lay round her shoulders, and her long golden hair was combed over the silk, straight and gleaming. Beside her, cross-legged on the floor, sat a tall man. A stranger.

Old, thought Cassy first. Not a boyfriend at all, but a man of fifty or more, with a lined, black face and a fringe of grizzled beard. And *thin*. Bony ankles and bare, long-toed feet. Long, long fingers, spread suddenly wide as he smiled at her out of the dark forest.

'Hallo, Little Red Riding Hood.'

For a moment she could not take her eyes off him. His narrow lips were taut round the dark cave of his mouth and his body was as tense as a hunting animal's, in the moment before it springs. He was waiting for some answer that she did not know how to give.

She put down her case and the bag, and tugged the hood back briskly, off her head. 'I'm Cassy,' she said. And then, to Goldie, 'Hallo, Mum.'

Goldie clapped her hands. 'Oh, Cassy! How lovely! I wanted you to come! Do you like my beautiful room?'

'Very nice,' Cassy said. She marched over to the mattress, delivered a firm, sensible kiss and suffered the strangling hug that Goldie always gave her.

This time it was shorter than usual. Goldie glanced past her, nervously watching the door. 'Where's Granny Phelan? You haven't left her downstairs, have you?'

'She's not here.' Cassy tried to ignore the smile and the way Goldie relaxed, suddenly, into the cushions. 'But she sent you a letter.' Unzipping her skirt pocket, she held out the envelope.

Goldie smiled again, but she made no effort to take the envelope. Instead, the man beside her leaned forward and tweaked it out of Cassy's hand.

'That's not for you—'

But he had ripped the letter open and was reading it, peering at the words in the half-light. As he reached the end, he snorted and looked up at Goldie, his face twisted with disgust.

'Does she always treat you like this?'

Goldie's smile faltered. 'Like what?'

'Giving orders.'

He jumped to his feet and read the letter aloud in a

grotesque, shrill voice, wagging his finger sternly at her. Round the room, a hundred other fingers wagged in time with it, exaggerating the mockery.

'You must keep Cassy with you until I send for her! Make sure she has proper food and clean clothes! Send her back when I write and say so!—No explanation. Nothing about money. No please or thank you.' He glared at the paper, then screwed it up and flung it into a corner. 'It's unbelievable! She just tells you what to do.'

Goldie smiled, vaguely, but Cassy felt like shouting. *You have to tell Goldie what to do! Or she'll just sit there and let the mess pile up round her*. This man must know that, if he lived with her.

He spun round suddenly and fixed his bright, dark eyes on Cassy. 'What's it all about? Why have you just turned up like this?'

Cassy stared back stubbornly. 'I don't know.'

'You don't know?' He raised his eyebrows and spread his hands wide. 'You mean—you woke up this morning and—wham!—you were sent off to stay with Goldie? Out of the blue?'

'That's right.'

'And you didn't ask why?'

'It's none of my business,' Cassy said flatly. Meaning, *It's none of yours*.

Goldie yawned. 'Don't fuss, Lyall, It's always like that. Cassy comes for a bit and then she goes away again. It's always happened, ever since she was old enough to walk and talk. Why should I mind? I *like* having her.'

'But you've never wondered about it?' Suddenly Lyall was very still, and the room was still with him.

'Why should I?' Goldie shrugged and smiled. 'Does it matter? She can stay, can't she?'

'Of course she can stay!' Lyall said impatiently. He strode to the door and bellowed, 'Robert!'

Feet thudded on the stairs and the boy was there in the doorway.

'Yes?'

'Cassy's staying.'

Lyall flung an arm round her shoulders, catching her off

16

balance. She staggered against him, feeling the ridged hardness of his ribs and the warmth of his body, and automatically she shrank away.

'What's the matter?' he said, glancing down at her. 'Tired?'

It was an easy excuse and more true than Cassy had realized. 'I've been travelling round and round looking for Goldie. All day.'

'Then you need a bed,' said Lyall. He waved a hand at Robert. 'Fix it up, Rob.'

'It's all done,' Robert said calmly. 'I've put the spare blankets in the front room downstairs.'

'Brilliant! Give her a hand with her bags, then.'

Robert picked up the suitcase in one hand and the shopping bag of food in the other and nodded at Cassy to show that she should follow him. She stepped out of the door and peered into the shadows on the stairs.

Robert was sure-footed in the dark, but she had to feel her way carefully. By the time she reached the bottom of the staircase he was already in the room at the front. She walked warily after him, prepared for more strangeness.

But it was an ordinary, empty room. Some blankets were piled on the bare boards and a fireplace gaped dustily in one wall. Robert had hooked an extra blanket across the bay window, but the upper panes were uncovered, letting in the dull glow of the street lamps. Automatically Cassy reached out and clicked the light switch.

Nothing happened.

'We're working on the electricity,' Robert said. Not apologetic, but proud. 'They won't connect us, but Lyall thinks he knows a way.'

Cassy smiled weakly, trying not to look disapproving, but Robert didn't seem to notice. He put down her bag and her case and went on with enthusiasm.

'It'll be a really good place if we get that. We've already got water. And a toilet down the hall that sort of works.'

'Oh,' said Cassy. She knew all about toilets like that.

'The kitchen's not very well organized, but we've got lots of food in. You're welcome to raid it, if you're hungry.'

'Not now, thanks.' But the mention of food reminded Cassy of the shopping bag. *Don't you go handing it over to Goldie*, Nan had said—but Robert was different. She picked up the bag and held it out. 'You ought to have this. It's some food that Nan sent, to help with my keep.'

'Great. Thanks.'

Robert took the bag and peered inside, spreading the handles wide. Cassy had a momentary glimpse of carrots and baked beans and tinned ham. And, at the very bottom, something smooth and yellow that she couldn't identify. (Bananas? But Nan wouldn't have put those under the tins.)

'Brilliant,' said Robert. He grinned and slung the bag over his arm. 'Anything else you want now?'

When Cassy shook her head, he padded off down the hall, towards the kitchen. Wearily she slid her feet out of her shoes and opened her suitcase to find the things she needed straightaway. Sponge bag. Pyjamas. Towel.

The photograph on top slid sideways and she caught it just before it hit the floor. It had better go on the mantelpiece at once, out of harm's way. She stood up and put it right in the middle, so that the solemn, boy's face stared down towards her makeshift bed. But not quite at it. However Cassy shifted the picture, she had never been able to make those eyes look at her.

They were still gazing across and beyond her as she settled under the blankets, wriggling to get herself comfortable on the hard floor. And when she closed her eyes, the solemn face jumbled with the rest of the day, making strange pictures as she sank into sleep.

* * *

. . . the sweet smell of pine trees was all round her and the ground under her feet was soft with needles. Layer upon layer upon layer.

There was no path through the forest. She turned slowly, gazing down alleys of trees. The lower branches barred her way, and the higher ones shut out the light.

The clearing was like a shout, raucous and shocking.

Bright blue sky. Bright green grass. And a patch of bright, bright yellow at the far edge. With the basket dragging at her arm, she began to push her way towards it, through the sharp branches.

The flowers sat close to the ground in their ruffs of frilled green leaves. Against the darkness of the pine trees, their yellow cups were as sharp as a challenge.

Winter aconites.

She stared at them, knowing—in her dream—that they had some other name. Some meaning that she needed to understand. But the word slid away like soap as she tried to grasp it and she could not remember.

She began to pick the flowers. . .

CHAPTER 3

And then she was awake. Quite suddenly, so that for a moment
the dream stayed with her and she could smell the sharp scent
of the pine needles.

As the forest faded, she opened her eyes to the bare room
with its peeling wallpaper and the blanket across the window.
It was bleak and dusty in the cold morning light, and her
breath hung in clouds in front of her.

She sat up and began to wriggle out of her blankets. The
moment she moved, she realized that she was ravenously
hungry. Unrolling her mac, which she had used as a pillow,
she stood up and pulled it on. Breakfast was what she needed.
She opened the door and stuck her head out into the hall.

Everything was very quiet upstairs, but someone seemed to
be moving around in the kitchen. There was a strong and
appetizing smell of frying. Cassy walked down the hall and
pushed open the kitchen door.

For a second she thought she was in the wrong place. She
had been expecting dirt, because Goldie's kitchens were always
filthy, but she hadn't expected rubbish and ruin. The room
looked as though it had been wrecked by a maniac.

Half the floor was covered with smashed wood, fragments of
lino and twisted pipes. All the kitchen fittings had been ripped
out systematically and left in a heap, with the broken sink on top.

The back door was barricaded. Heavy strips of wood had
been nailed across the frame and dozens of plastic bags and
cardboard boxes were stacked in front of it. Even from the
doorway, Cassy could smell stale cabbage leaves and rotten
meat.

The only permanent, fixed thing was a tap. It hung in the
air, about half a metre above the ground, attached to a new
copper pipe that stuck up from the floor. In front was a plastic
bowl with a dirty cloth in it, placed to catch drips.

Taking another step, Cassy saw the stove. It was a small gas camping stove, standing in one corner, on the floor. There was a black frying pan on top, with four rashers of bacon arranged in it. Robert was kneeling beside the stove, turning the bacon with a knife.

'Hallo,' Cassy said.

He looked up. 'You're an early riser, are you? A bit different from Goldie.'

Cassy imagined the list in his head.

Early risers: Robert Cornelius and Cathleen Phelan.

Late risers: Susan Phelan (and Lyall Cornelius?).

'No point in lying around,' she said. 'Not when there's things to do. Is there something I can have for breakfast?'

Robert looked at the four rashers of bacon. 'I'll put some fried bread in.'

He settled his knife on the edge of the frying pan and went to the nearest cardboard box to fetch the bread. Cassy pulled a face, thinking of food and rubbish side by side. But she knew what Nan would have done, so she did it.

Marching across the kitchen, she grabbed two of the nearest rubbish bags. 'Is there somewhere outside where I can put these?'

'The kerb.' Robert was busy fitting slices of bread into the frying pan. 'The dustmen come today. But you needn't bother. I was going to do it after breakfast anyway.'

Cassy ignored the last part and began to heave the rubbish sacks down the hall and out on to the pavement. She put them in the gutter, in front of the Moongazer van, and went back for more. By the time the fried bread was ready, she had made a tidy heap in the road. Four black plastic bags and two soggy boxes. Brushing off her hands she marched back into the kitchen.

Robert was lifting bread and bacon on to a plate. He glanced curiously at her. 'You may be small, but you're pretty tough, aren't you? Goldie would never have shifted those sacks. You're not much like her, are you?'

'Of course not!' Cassy took the plate as he held it out and settled herself down on the floor. 'Thanks very much.'

Robert shrugged. 'It's not exactly a feast. But it'll—keep the wolf from the door.'

He spoke the last words with a strange emphasis, like some kind of joke, but it obviously wasn't a joke for Cassy to share. She made a neat sandwich with her bacon and fried bread and glanced at the battered kettle beside Robert. 'Any chance of a cup of tea?'

'Sure.' He picked up the kettle and turned on the tap. The water came out in a great rush that set the pipe juddering. Putting the frying pan down on the floor, he balanced the heavy kettle on the little stove. 'Sorry there's no chairs. We've only been here two or three weeks and we've had a lot to get straight.'

'What sort of things?' As far as Cassy could see, they had spent all their time sticking up bits of mirror.

Robert put his sandwich down in the frying pan and began to tick things off on his fingers. 'Floorboards. Half of them were ripped up, to stop people using the house—Lyall almost fell down to the cellar when we first broke in. Roof. That was leaking quite badly. Water. We had to connect that before we moved in, because Goldie wanted a proper toilet.'

'Of course she did!'

Robert grinned. 'When we moved into the Wandsworth squat, the toilet was blocked up with concrete. And we had so many shows booked that we couldn't clear it for two weeks.' He took another bite of bacon and fried bread.

Cassy made herself go on eating, but she changed the subject. 'Shows? What sort of shows?'

'In schools, of course. Moongazer shows.' Robert looked at her. 'Don't you know what we do?'

'Of course I don't. I'd never even heard of you until I got here.'

'Well—' Robert looked down at his feet for a moment, eating steadily, before he went on. 'Lyall runs workshops— mostly in schools. Drama workshops, writing workshops, *thinking* workshops. It's hard to explain exactly what they are, but they're absolutely fantastic.'

'And Goldie works with him?' Cassy couldn't imagine Goldie in a thinking workshop.

'Sometimes she does. And I do as well, if he needs me. But mostly I do the research and keep track of the bookings and the money and all his tax.'

'But how do you have time? What about school?'

'I don't go to school much.' Robert grinned again. 'Only when they catch up with me.'

'But—'

'School's a waste of time. I've been running the business side of Moongazer for nearly three years now. On my own, more or less. You don't get that at school.'

'But there's other things—'

'Sure there are. Want to know what I've researched for Lyall so far?' He held up his finger again, making another list. 'South American history: in detail. Polar exploration: loads of scientific stuff in that one. Jungles: that was science *and* history *and* economics *and* world politics. And the thing I'm working on now spreads even wider than that.'

Cassy blinked at the volley of words, but he did not give her time to recover.

'I bet you don't know what a *ligahoo* is. Or what the Anglo-Saxons called January. Or what happened to Monsieur Seguin's goat. Do you?'

'I—'

'What spider ambushes its prey instead of spinning a web? What moth do you find in granaries?'

'That's not education,' Cassy said. 'Those are just little, isolated facts.'

'Oh no they're not!' Robert looked triumphant. 'They're not isolated at all. They're all linked to the same thing.'

He leaned close, waving his sandwich in the air.

'It seemed like a narrow subject when we started, but it covers millions of things. Big ones—ecology and history and the nature of fear—and silly little details as well.' He waved the sandwich again, hunting for an example. 'Like the folk names for sun spurge and club moss and winter aconite.'

Winter aconite. Something twanged at the back of Cassy's mind and, for a second, she stopped hearing Robert's voice. Her mind was chasing a memory that slid away faster than she could catch at it. A threatening, uneasy memory. *Winter aconites* . . .

Suddenly she didn't want to know what Robert was talking about. Shying away from the conversation, she glanced quickly round the kitchen and saw Nan's old shopping bag, tipped on to its side.

'Shall I take that away?' she said, abruptly. 'Is it empty?'

Robert blinked, his mind still on club moss and the nature of fear. Then he sprawled across the room and pulled the bag towards him. 'It's almost empty. But I didn't know what that stuff at the bottom was.'

'What stuff? I thought it was all food.'

Robert opened the bag and held it out for her to see. At the bottom, roughly wrapped in a piece of newspaper, was a solid lump of—something. One corner of the newspaper had fallen away, showing the smooth yellow patch that had puzzled Cassy the night before.

Reaching into the basket, she lifted out the bundle and pulled the newspaper away. The lump inside looked like Plasticine or marzipan, except that the colour was brighter. She prodded at it with one finger. It had a faintly oily surface.

'I thought it must have got in there by mistake,' Robert said. 'What is it?'

Cassy prodded again and the substance gave slightly, as though it could be moulded. 'I don't know,' she said slowly. 'I've never seen it before.'

'It must belong to your grandmother, mustn't it? Do you think she wants it back, or is it just a bit of old junk?'

Cassy frowned down at it. 'Nan doesn't have bits of old junk. She's not like that. I can't imagine how it got into the bag.'

'Can't you phone her up and ask?'

'But we haven't got a phone, and I can't bother—'

I can't bother Mrs Ramage, she meant to say. But somehow the words wouldn't come out. Sitting in that wrecked kitchen, with its dirty floor and its sour smells, she suddenly wanted, unbearably to talk to Nan.

Slowly, she ran her finger over the smooth yellow surface of the lump on her lap. She hadn't looked for an excuse to phone. It had come to her. Surely Nan would understand that.

'Where's the nearest phone box?' she said abruptly.

'Up to the main road and turn left. Want me to come?'

'No thanks. I'll be fine. Shall I wash up my plate?'

Robert shook his head, gathering the plates and frying pan

together with quick, efficient hands. 'I'm quite used to washing up. I usually do it all. You go and make your phone call.'

Scooping the yellow lump into Nan's bag, Cassy carried it off to her room. There was no point in wasting time wondering what it was. She stood the bag in a corner and began to dress as quickly as she could, surprised at her own impatience.

Twenty minutes later she was standing in the phone box, dialling Mrs Ramage's number. As she waited for an answer, she rattled her fingernails against the glass and when the ringing stopped she spoke at once. 'Mrs Ramage? It's Cassy, from next door.'

'Cassy?' Mrs Ramage was old and slow and she took a long time to work things out. 'Where are you then, dear?'

'I'm in a phone box.' It was no use trying to explain 'Would you mind—could you possibly fetch Nan for me? I need to speak to her.'

'Well, I haven't seen her around for a day or two—'

'Please, Mrs Ramage. I'll ring off and phone back in a few minutes, shall I?'

'Yes, dear. You do that. I'll go and fetch her for you.'

Mrs Ramage put the phone down and Cassy stared through the glass at the dull grey sky. How long should she wait? Five minutes? Ten? Mrs Ramage didn't walk very fast.

After seven minutes she put in some more money and tapped in the number again. This time, the phone was answered at the first ring.

'Nan?'

'What?' said Mrs Ramage's voice.

'Oh. Is Nan out?'

'No dear, she's *in*. But she said to tell you she was very busy. And she sent you her best love.'

'She wouldn't come?' For a moment Cassy couldn't make sense of the words. She wouldn't have bothered Mrs Ramage unless it was important. Nan must have guessed that. So why—? 'Is she ill?'

'Oh, I don't think so. She looked quite well to me.'

'And she wouldn't come?' Cassy said again.

'I told you, dear.' Mrs Ramage began to sound faintly impatient. 'She said, *Tell her I'm perfectly well and not to worry, but I'm a bit tied up just now. Give her my best love and say I'm looking forward to getting a postcard.'*

'Oh.'

'Is that all right then? Or was there something else?'

'No . . . no.' Cassy gathered her wits. 'Thank you very much for going round. I'm sorry to have troubled you.'

'No trouble, dear. Any time. Goodbye.'

'Goodbye.'

Very carefully, Cassy put the receiver back into place. Then she stepped out into the cold air and took three deep breaths. *The world doesn't have to explain itself to you*—that was what Nan always said. All she needed to know about was the yellow stuff. And if that were important, surely Nan would have come to the phone.

But something else fretted at her as she walked back to Albert Street, with her face turned fiercely into the wind. It was only as she reached the house that she worked out what it was.

Nan shouldn't have been there at all. Not if she was perfectly well. It was only Tuesday—even though Monday seemed a lifetime away—and that meant she was still on early. She ought to have left the flat at six o'clock.

CHAPTER 4

Two strange things. The yellow stuff and Nan. Cassy was still wondering about them when she got back to the house.

'Did you find it OK?' Robert said, as he opened the door.

'What?' Cassy said vaguely. 'Oh yes, thank you.'

He stepped back to let her in. 'And what's the stuff? Is it important?'

'She—'

For an instant, Cassy was on the verge of telling him all about it. Asking him what he thought. But how could he understand when he had never met Nan? He didn't know how reliable and unchanging she was, and he must be used to much stranger things. Being Lyall's son.

'No, it's nothing important,' she muttered. 'But thanks for saving it.'

She gave him an absent-minded smile and went into her bedroom, shutting the door behind her. Then she opened her suitcase and found the neat packet of white postcards. It was certainly time to send Nan one of those. Nan still thought that Goldie was living in the bedsit in Notting Hill and that Cassy was with her. Instead of which—

Cassy looked down at the blank side of the postcard and shook her head. How could she fit everything on to that? She had only been one day away, but she could have written pages. About hunting for Goldie. About the house. About Lyall and Robert. But all that would have to wait for the next postcard, or the one after that. This time she had to concentrate on what was really important.

Her new address. *Never put your own address on a postcard,* Nan said. *It's just a waste of space.* But this was different, of course. Nan had to have her new address, so that she could tell her when to come home. Cassy made sure that she wrote it large and clear.

Everything else had to be squashed together underneath. It sounded very jerky, but it was the best she could manage.

> *This is a squat. Goldie is living with a man called Lyall and his son Robert. She's working(!!) It's not too bad. A bit messy. What shall I do with the yellow stuff that was in the food bag? See you soon. Love, Cassy.*

As she was writing her name at the bottom, she heard feet on the stairs.

'Cassy!' Goldie flung the door open and looked round it. 'Oh *there* you are! Hurry up, or you'll be late.'

'Late for what?'

'Making the masks, of course!' Goldie danced into the room. 'I *am* pleased you've come! It's lovely having you here to join in.'

She flung her arms wide, and Cassy shrank away from the hug.

'What masks? What are you talking about?'

But Goldie had taken a step backwards and bumped into Nan's shopping bag. It fell over, and immediately her mind jumped to something else.

'What's this yellow stuff, Cassy? Is it yours?'

Cassy pushed it back into the bag, out of sight. 'Mum! What about the masks?'

'What? Oh yes!' Goldie said, brightening. 'You must come and help.'

Cassy gave up trying to talk sense. 'I'll come in a minute. I've just got to go to the post.'

'Oh, no!' Goldie pouted. 'It's miles and miles to the postbox. And we've got ever such a lot of work to do.'

It was like arguing with a nagging child. Goldie never gave up once she had an idea in her head. If Cassy set off down the road, she would probably follow, tugging at her sleeve.

'Oh—all right. Hang on a minute.' Cassy pushed the postcard into her mac pocket, ready to post when she next went out. Then she picked up the bag and stood it neatly beside her suitcase and the folded blankets. The room might be bare, but it didn't have to be untidy.

'Aren't you coming?' Goldie said, from the doorway.

'I'm ready now.' Cassy followed her, shut the door and clattered up the stairs.

She had expected the others to be in the mirror room, but Goldie led her straight past the open door. The mirrors were lifeless in the dusty daylight and the draped cloth looked shabby. There was nothing left of last night's magic forest.

The front bedroom was completely different. It was the biggest room, stretching right across the front of the house, and someone obviously slept in one corner. There was a sleeping bag laid out tidily on a pile of folded blankets.

But the sleeping bag was walled off from the rest of the room by a neat row of cardboard boxes. Each one had a label stuck to the side, decorated with a picture of long legs, like the ones on the van. Over the legs arched the same word. MOONGAZER.

The main part of the room was used as a workshop. A roll of chicken wire stood in one corner, next to a box full of tools. Next to it, four half finished masks were lined up under the window. They were made of papier mâché, on a base of chicken wire, but it was hard to guess what they were meant to be. The papier mâché was still rough and the printed words, criss-crossing at random, confused Cassy's eye and disguised the shapes.

In the centre of the floor was a heap of newspaper. Lyall and Robert were sitting beside it, shredding the pages into neat strips and dropping them into a bucket. As Goldie and Cassy walked through the door, Lyall jumped up, in one energetic, fluid movement. He bounded towards them, with his arms held out.

'Have we got a new recruit? Are you going to help us, Cassy?'

'I—' Cassy took a step backwards, as though he might engulf her. 'What do you want me to do?'

'You could help me tear up the paper,' Robert began, but Lyall held up a hand.

'She's not slave labour! We want her to *share*—and she can't do that until she understands. Read all about us, Cassy!'

Cassy would rather have torn up paper, with Robert, but she smiled politely and took the leaflet that Lyall held out. Goldie beamed.

'It's the most fantastic thing! Moongazing! I like it best in the whole, wide world!' She stretched out her arms and spun round the room on tiptoe until she was dizzy and Lyall had to catch her.

Cassy looked at the leaflet. On the front was a photograph of Lyall, in a scarlet tracksuit. He was standing under a tree and the photograph had been taken from ground level, so that his legs and feet were huge and his head was impossibly small and far away. He seemed to tower up and up, into the tree and towards the clouds. MOONGAZER said the black letters, printed in an arch above the picture.

Inside, the leaflet was full of smaller, more ordinary photographs. All of them showed Lyall with different groups of children. In some, his face was exotically painted. He was a clown, a tiger, a monster with glaring eyes. In other pictures, it was the children who were disguised and Lyall who was watching.

> *Open new windows!* began the writing round the pictures. *A day with MOONGAZER will have children acting and writing and thinking as they've never done before.*

> *The whole world is his treasury. He combines history, science, literature and much, much more, drawing on the riches of Europe, the culture of the Caribbean, the wisdom of Africa and the mysteries of Asia.*

> *MOONGAZER has worked as an actor, a teacher, a potter and a musician. His amazing talents reach their peak in the work that he brings to schools and festivals, book weeks and play schemes.*

> *For further details. . .*

Cassy's glance jumped to the last picture of all. It showed two opposing groups of children. One group was led by Lyall, with a big wooden cross in his hand. The other group was led by Goldie. She was holding a golden sun-disc, with twisted, stylized rays, and she looked like a warrior angel.

Play-acting, thought Cassy. She ought to have guessed that Goldie wouldn't be doing real work.

When she looked up, she met Lyall's eyes. He was standing perfectly still, watching her, and his expression was sharp and shrewd. She had summed him up as a clown, a man who leapt about and played games, but there was nothing clownish about the way he was looking at her. She wondered, uncomfortably, if her thoughts about the leaflet had shown in her face.

'It's very interesting,' she said quickly, giving it back to him. 'What can I do to help?'

Lyall waved at Robert. 'How about helping him with the papier mâché? It's the last layer, but we're making four masks, so we need a lot.'

'Me too,' Goldie said, dropping to the floor beside Robert. 'I like doing papier mâché, even if it does make my fingers black.'

'And no one tears the paper as small as you do.'

Lyall swooped down to kiss the top of her head and Cassy turned away. Picking up a thick bundle of papers, she ripped them across, in half and in half again, so that they tore jaggedly into irregular pieces.

'Not like that.' Robert held up his own paper to demonstrate. 'It's better to get a rhythm going. Then all the bits turn out the same size, more or less. Watch Goldie. She's brilliant at it. Better than a machine.'

'That's because she turns her brain off while she does it,' said Lyall. He was crouching in the corner now, behind the chicken wire, but he grinned over his shoulder. 'You're good at turning your brain off, aren't you, Goldie?'

Goldie stuck her tongue out at him. 'You think I'm so stupid, don't you, Lyall Cornelius? But *I'm* the one who thought of this new show. Aren't I? It was absolutely all my own idea, and you said it was brilliant. Better than all *your* ideas. Or Robert's.'

'And so it is,' Lyall said. 'It's the best idea we've ever had. I can't think how it came out of that empty head of yours.'

Goldie gave a delighted, outraged yelp, threw her newspapers at him and bounded across the room. Flinging herself after the newspapers, she landed on top of Lyall and began to tickle him fiercely, while he laughed and struggled and Robert called out to them both.

'Mind the masks, you idiots! We'll never get ready in time for Friday if you squash them!'

Cassy didn't know what to do, or where to look. How *could*

they? Goldie was grown up—even if she was odd—and Lyall was *old*. But they were behaving like a pair of children. She tried to ignore them, but that was impossible, because Lyall was screeching 'Mercy! Mercy!' at the top of his voice, and Goldie was laughing hysterically.

It was stupid to let her get like that. Couldn't Lyall see? *Goldie's all right as long as she doesn't get excited*, Nan said. *As long as she's calm, she's quite good at doing what you tell her.* But she was completely out of control now. No one would ever be able to stop her.

As if he had read Cassy's mind, Robert stood up. Stepping across the room, without any hurry, he grabbed the back of Goldie's jumper and pulled her off Lyall.

'You're going to squash the masks, Goldie,' he said. Perfectly quietly and kindly. 'And you'll be sorry when you've done it.'

Lyall stood up and Goldie sat back on her heels, giggling weakly. 'Give in,' she said. 'Go on, Lyall.'

'I give in,' he said solemnly.

'Say I'm brilliant.'

'I'm brilliant,' Lyall said. Then, as Goldie screwed up her fists and growled, he ducked his head. 'No, no, I mean you're brilliant of course, Goldie dear.'

'And my idea is the best idea *ever*?'

Cassy couldn't stand the nonsense any more. 'What is this brilliant idea, anyway?' she said. 'No one's told me yet.'

'You mean—you don't know?' Lyall flung his hands up in wild, exaggerated astonishment. 'I thought Robert would have made you sick of the word, already.'

'What word?' Cassy thought she would go mad if she had to live with Lyall very long.

'*What* word, she says!' Lyall shrugged elaborately and rolled his eyes towards the ceiling. 'As if the house didn't ring with it, all day long. As if Robert didn't murmur it in his sleep and write it in golden syrup in his porridge every morning. As if—'

'Knock it off, Lyall,' Robert muttered. 'You can see she's not used to being wound up like that. It's not fair.' He was still ripping paper, steadily and evenly, amid all the chaos. Without stopping, he turned to Cassy. 'What we're doing is—Wolves.'

Wolves—and winter aconite . . .

'Not *Wolves*,' Lyall said impatiently. 'That sounds like some kind of nature talk. It's *Wolf*, boy. That's what we're doing.' He spun round and grabbed one of the masks from the floor behind him. It was an awkward, ungainly shape, about a metre long, with faces from newspaper photographs spattered distractingly all over it. He waved it at Cassy. 'Look.'

Cassy looked, but all she could see was something like a giant, lumpy sausage, which widened out into a mask shape at one end.

'Wolves don't look like that,' she said.

'Exactly!' Lyall beamed, as though she had said something clever. '*Wolves* don't look like that. But *Wolf*—' and he beamed again, leaving the sentence unfinished.

Cassy hadn't got the faintest idea what he was talking about, but she wasn't going to ask. She had had quite enough of Lyall for the time being. Bending her head, she began to tear up newspaper, concentrating on the size of her strips and not taking any notice of anything else.

But later in the day—much later—the conversation came back to her, teasing her mind. As she lay down in her blankets that night, she wondered why she had been so sure. *Wolves don't look like that.* How did she know? What had she ever had to do with wolves?

She tried to make some kind of picture in her mind, but the image slid about shapelessly, splitting into disconnected fragments. A gaping, murderous mouth. Long yellow fangs. Sharp ears, lifted or laid back—

What *did* a wolf look like?

The question irritated her so much that she sat up and reached for her suitcase. She meant to find a pen and a piece of paper, so that she could try to draw the wretched animal.

But her hand touched the shopping bag instead of the case. It toppled towards her in the dark, spilling out the solid lump inside in its newspaper wrapping.

That would do. Better than paper, in fact, if she could really mould it. She began to work at it with her fingers, gradually softening it as she pinched and pulled and squeezed.

She needed a body, strong and deep at the chest and

narrowing towards the rear. Four legs. A tail. And a head with pricked ears, turning slightly upwards, towards the moon.

Her fingers struggled, moulding and re-moulding, trying to find the exact shape that would answer the image in her mind, the shape that would mean *Wolf*. How did it go? Heavy and threatening? Or wider here? Or was it more delicate altogether, with a fine, narrow muzzle?

Long before she found a shape that satisfied her, she slid sideways on to the blankets and slept.

* * *

. . . the yellow flowers of the aconite lay scattered over the checked cloth on her basket. It was a red and white cloth, moulded into hills and valleys by the shapes underneath. The smooth hump of the new loaf. The circular tops of the custard cups. The long, smooth rod of the bottle's neck.

She stood with her back to a tree, in that stillness which makes movement impossible in dreams.

Where are you going? Can I show you the way?

The whispering voice caressed her ear, familiar but unrecognized. She could not turn to see who had spoken, and her mind danced away, refusing to make a picture of the face. But she knew the huskiness, and the warm breath, and the slow, enticing murmur that went on and on.

Shall I show you the path? We could play a little game . . .

CHAPTER 5

'No!' Cassy said. '*No!*'

She woke instantly, wondering why she had spoken. Had there been a question . . . ?

But the dream had gone, leaving only the uneasy prickling of her skin. Stupid to take any notice of that. The best remedy for peculiar feelings was to be up and doing.

Scrambling out of her blankets, she gathered up the top one and shook it, hard, getting ready to fold it. Something fell from the blanket on to the floor, landing on the boards with a soft, almost noiseless thud. Cassy bent to pick it up.

It was the yellow lump that she had been trying to mould into a wolf shape. There was nothing wolfish about it now. She must have rolled on it in her sleep, because it was squashed out of all recognition, into a strange distorted shape like the map of an unknown continent. Or like—

Turning it over in her hands, she tried to think of a better comparison, but she could not concentrate. Nan's voice seemed to be ringing in her ears. *Up and doing. You don't want to waste time mooning about.*

Squashing the shape together quickly, into a rough ball, Cassy put it up on the mantelpiece, beside the photograph of her father. Then she dressed, tidied her blankets and went down the hall.

She could hear Robert, already moving around in the kitchen. He was up and doing too, was he? So much the better. There were plenty of things for them to sort out and two people could get through a lot more than one. Perhaps she could persuade him to get on with clearing the kitchen this morning. She hoped the kettle was already on.

'Hallo!' she said brightly, striding into the kitchen.

The kettle was certainly on, but Robert wasn't ready to start clearing the kitchen. He looked up at her from the middle of a sea of papers. There was a box file open in front of him and all round, in neat little piles, were newspaper cuttings and pages covered with close, neat writing.

'Whatever are you doing?'

Cassy glanced down at the nearest pile and she had her answer before Robert could say a word. There, gazing up at her, was a wolf.

It stood alert, in a blur of green shadows, its pale black-rimmed eyes staring sharp and cold. The speckled coat spread in a ruff around the triangle of its face and its ears stood erect. Below the photograph, a headline screamed.

WOLF EXPLOSION IN SPAIN
Wolves return to Cantabria
Farmers in the 'Picos de Europa'—Spain's 'Alps'—are up in arms about the sudden increase in the wolf population . . .

'Wolves,' Cassy said slowly, looking round.

Robert grinned. 'I know it's a mess, but that's because I'm putting it all in order. We've got a booking next Monday and Lyall wants to try this out.'

'Try what out?' said Cassy. How could all those tatty scraps of paper turn into a show?

She squatted down, peering more closely at the little piles. There were photographs of wolves. Maps and charts to show how many wolves lived where and at what time in history. A long book list, with most of the books ticked off. And a coloured wallchart of *How Wolves Communicate*, with dozens of wolfish faces, threatening or cringing or grinning.

Disconnected snippets danced up at her, listed in careful handwriting.

wolf   *(Eng.)*
loup   *(Fr.)*
lupus   *(Lat.)*
λŭkos   *(Gk.)*
lobo   *(Span.)*
lobo   *(Port.)*

No matter how much you feed a wolf, he will always return to the forest (Russian)
The wolf loses his teeth, but not his inclinations (Spanish)
The wolf is kept fed by his feet (Russian)

> wolfmonath—*January (Anglo-Saxon)*
> wolf-spider —*ambushes prey instead of spinning a web*
> wolfsmilk   —*sun spurge*
> wolf's claw —*club moss*
> wolf-bane —*winter aconite*
> wolf's head —*outlaw*

Cassy looked away, towards the untidiest pile of all. Different-sized pieces of paper were shuffled together, and they all seemed to be drawings. Some in ink, some in pencil, some in felt pen. She bent and picked up the top picture, trying to make sense of it.

A huge black circle had been scrawled in the very centre of the paper and roughly shaded in. Round the edge of the circle were jagged triangular shapes, some pointing inwards and some pointing outwards. The triangles had been drawn so fiercely that, in one or two places, the pen had gone right through the paper.

'That's Lyall's favourite,' Robert said.

It would be, Cassy thought. She shook her head. 'I must be stupid. I can't even see what it's meant to be.'

'Wolf, of course.'

'Wolf?' Cassy looked at him, to see whether he was joking. 'But it's nothing like a wolf.'

'Not *a* wolf,' Robert said patiently. 'We've got lots of photographs of those. This is something quite different. Lyall said "Wolf"—and then he got people to draw the picture that came into their head. Goldie drew that one—the big gaping mouth with the terrible teeth. Lyall was thrilled to bits.'

'Oh, it's Goldie's, is it?'

Cassy put it to the bottom of the heap and went on leafing through. There were about thirty pictures. Wolves running or leaping or baying the moon. Long-muzzled wolves that belonged in cartoons, and long-legged wolves that looked more like horses. She picked out the most sensible one she could find. A proper wolf, with a head and a body and a tail, and four legs. Shaded in pencil, so that you could almost feel its fur.

'*That*'s what a wolf looks like,' she said, holding it up for Robert to see.

He frowned. 'You haven't really got the idea.' He slid a paper-clip on to the cuttings he was sorting and put them on the floor. 'Earl did that drawing—our friend from the Wandsworth squat. He's a painter and he does lots of work for Moongazer. Lyall was looking forward to his wolf picture. He was furious when Earl gave him that.'

'*Furious?*'

'He said "You're holding out on me, Earl. That's just a wolf from the zoo you've drawn. Not the wolf inside you."'

'The what?' Cassy snorted and put the drawings down on the floor again. 'That's just nonsense. Wolves are wolves, and people are people.'

'It's not quite as simple as that.' Robert looked earnest and pompous, as if he were giving a lecture. 'The way we think about wolves is twisted up with the way we think about ourselves. We've been linked for thousands of years. Perhaps for millions.'

A thin streak of steam began to rise from the kettle's spout, giving Cassy an excuse to move. Stepping round and past and over all the wolf-pictures and wolf-writings, she picked up the teapot and tossed in a couple of teabags.

'I haven't got a clue what you're talking about.'

'Well—look at this, for example.' Robert flapped yet another sheet of paper at her. 'Is that about wolves? Or about people?'

Cassy looked down at the closely-written notes.

WEREWOLVES

1. *France: 'Loup garou'   Caribbean: 'Ligahoo', or 'lagahoo'*
2. *Europe: M. Ages mostly. Esp. France. People BELIEVED they changed into wolves and killed others. (Hallucinations from eating ergot fungus or rye? Or survival of primitive totemistic religion— Wolf Clan?)*

3. *W.wolves turn skins inside out to show hairy underside. Or wear wolfskin belts. Or change shape at full moon. Some can't help it.*
4. *Cure: (a) steal their hidden clothes (b) shoot with silver bullet. N.B. human body has same wound as wolf body.*
5. *Grip of w.wolf's teeth unbreakable, even after death. Mouthful must be cut out and buried with them.*

'*Werewolves?* Oh, for heavens sake!' Cassy picked up the kettle and poured a steady stream of boiling water into the teapot. 'You sit there dreaming about horror stories if you like. I'm going to clear up this kitchen. And I'm going to wake Goldie up and tell her to help me.'

'I don't think Lyall would like you to—'

'I don't care what Lyall would like. I'm not going to live like a pig.'

Briskly, Cassy picked up four open milk cartons, one after another. She sniffed them, chose the least nasty and hunted round for some mugs. When she had swilled the mugs out with the rest of the hot water, she poured three lots of tea. One for Robert, one for herself and one for Goldie.

'There you are,' she said. 'I'll come down and have some bread when I've woken Goldie. Then you'd better go and work somewhere else. Unless you're going to help us.'

Robert took the mug she handed to him, but he didn't say anything except, 'Thank you.' By the time Cassy had reached the door, he was already concentrating on his papers again.

Stupid nonsense! Fancy wasting your life on that while everything fell to pieces all round you! Cassy strode up the stairs and knocked on the mirror room door.

Two quick taps. And then—after a pause—another two quick taps, to make sure.

Somewhere, at the back of her head, the rhythm of her knocking echoed like a half-remembered tune, but she ignored it. She'd had enough fancies for one morning. She wanted to wake Goldie up and start on the work.

But there was still no noise from inside the room. Impatiently, Cassy tapped again, calling softly. 'Mum?'

She heard a rustling, like the sound of someone sitting up in bed. Then Lyall's puzzled voice.

'Goldie? What's the matter?'

There was a shuffle. Feet walked very fast across the bare boards and Lyall flung the door open. He was wearing nothing but a pair of shorts and he loomed huge and dark as he glowered down at Cassy.

'What the hell is going on?'

She stepped back. 'I brought Goldie a cup of tea.'

'Some cup of tea! What have you done to her?'

Lyall pointed into the corner of the room. Goldie was sitting bolt upright on the mattress, staring at the door with wide eyes. All around her, dusty mirrors caught the image of her silky nightdress, sliding off one shoulder, and her wild, tangled hair. She seemed to be rigid with shock.

'Goldie?' said Cassy. 'Mum?'

Goldie blinked, looked round and blinked again. 'It's you, Cassy?' Slowly she shook her head from side to side. 'But I heard—I thought—'

Lyall loped across the room and laid a hand on her head. 'You just had a bad dream. OK? Because Cassy woke you up so suddenly.'

'It wasn't a dream!' Goldie said pettishly, shaking his hand away. 'I wasn't even asleep. I was lying here, watching the sun on the mirrors. And then I heard—' She looked down at her hands and they twisted together, tangling the bedclothes.

'Heard what?' Lyall said. And then, more fiercely, 'Heard *who*?'

Goldie's mumbled answer was so soft that Cassy could hardly make out the words. 'It was Mick. I heard Mick, knocking on the bedroom door.'

Cassy caught her breath. Just hearing that name, spoken out loud, was like a punch in the stomach. *Mick Phelan*. Before she could recover, Lyall had rounded on her, shouting.

'What did you do? Were you playing some kind of trick?'

'Of course I wasn't!' Cassy snapped. 'I just knocked. Because I thought she ought to wake up and help me clear the kitchen. I think it's time someone—'

'How did you knock?'

'Oh—I don't know.' She frowned, hesitated and then knocked twice on the door behind her. 'Like that, I think. And then again, to make sure she heard.'

She gave another quick double knock, to demonstrate, and Goldie leaned forward and banged a fist down on the mattress.

'There you are! I told you I wasn't dreaming. That's Mick's special knock. His signal.'

Lyall glared at Cassy and opened his mouth, but she interrupted before he could say anything.

'That's nothing to do with me. I've never seen him—not since I was a baby. Nan doesn't even talk about him. How could I have known about any special knock?'

Once again, for a second, the rhythm of that knock echoed at the back of her mind, but she couldn't pin it down. As soon as she tried to remember, it slid teasingly away. Cassy held out the mug of tea to Goldie.

'Do you want this, or shall I take it away?'

Lyall lifted it out of her hands. 'You ought to drink it, Goldie. You've had a bit of a shock, I think. It'll help to calm you down. Come on—'

Turning away, Cassy left them to it and headed for the stairs. But before she was halfway down, Lyall came running after her, putting an arm round her shoulders.

'Hey, look,' he muttered. 'I'm sorry I yelled at you. I should have guessed it was just one of Goldie's illusions. She's always doing that.'

Cassy wriggled away from the arm. 'Doing what?'

'Thinking she hears *him*. Or sees him, or smells his aftershave or—' He leaned back against the banisters, with his eyes closed and his mouth twisted. 'Why can't I just get used to it?'

Cassy wanted to run, before he could say another word, but she made herself answer lightly, as though she hadn't noticed his face. 'Like the boy who cried "Wolf"?'

The eyes opened, one at a time, and the mouth unwound into a smile. 'I hope not. You know how *that* story ends.'

'You mean—?'

'I mean the real wolf came along at last.'

This time the face he pulled was comically grotesque and,

41

for a moment, Cassy almost liked him. But before she could say anything, Goldie called from the mirror room and immediately he turned and ran back to her.

Fussing! Cassy snorted and walked downstairs to begin clearing the kitchen. But his last words rang unnervingly in her ears.

The real wolf came along at last . . .

CHAPTER 6

Work emptied her mind. For the rest of the morning, Cassy was too busy to think about wolves. Or Nan, or strange yellow substances. All she had time for was splintered wood and dirty, broken lino.

By lunchtime, she was halfway down the heap. All on her own, she had carried the broken rubbish round the outside of the house, through the alley and down to the bottom of the garden. At first it annoyed her that no one came to help, but gradually the rhythm of the work took over and she let herself enjoy what she was doing. Clearing up mess. Making things neat and tidy.

And then Lyall shouted at her.

'What are you doing *now*?'

It was like thunder. He was leaning out of the back bedroom window, booming at her, and his face was furious. Cassy dropped her armful of wood and took a step backwards. Her hands shook, but she wasn't going to be terrified. She yelled back at him, even more loudly.

'I'm clearing out the kitchen. I don't like living in a slum. The whole lot's coming out here, and then I'm going to have a bonfire.'

Lyall looked even more furious. 'You want the neighbours to go mad? You want them to try and get us out? If we light a bonfire like that, they'll be phoning up the council in droves.'

'But—'

'It's a smokeless zone. And we're trying to be neighbourly and acceptable, you little fool.'

'But we can't just live like—'

'Don't be so bloody officious. Get inside.'

Lyall slammed the window so hard that the glass shook. Cassy shook too, with rage and frustration—and something very like fear.

Why did he have to make everything so fierce and intense? Why couldn't he—?

Cassy couldn't think what she wanted Lyall to do, but she knew that it was no use doing any more clearing. He would yell at her again and they would end up fighting. She had to get out. To go for a walk or something.

Running up the garden, she marched through the alley— and straight into Goldie's arms.

Goldie was dancing on the pavement, dressed up to go out, with an emerald-green scarf over her coat and a green beret perched on her head. As Cassy came out of the alley, she gave a long gurgle of delight.

'Ooooh, brilliant! You can come with us!' Grabbing Cassy's arm, she called out at the top of her voice. 'Lyall, Lyall! Get Cassy's coat. She's going to come with us.'

'No I'm not,' muttered Cassy. 'Let me go.' She tried to pull free, but Goldie just laughed and grabbed her other arm as well.

'Don't be silly, Cassy. It's going to be fun. We've got sandwiches for lunch, and Lyall's got an appointment, and—'

'Let go!' Cassy said. But she couldn't get free without fighting Goldie and that was impossible. In public, in the street.

And then it was too late. Lyall was coming down the path, with a carrier bag in one hand and Cassy's mac in the other. He threw them both into the back of the Moongazer van and then opened the front door with a grin at Cassy. As though he hadn't just been bawling her out.

'I'm sure you can squash in the middle. Earl does, and he's twice your size.'

'But I'm not—'

It was useless to say anything. Ten seconds later, without quite knowing how it had happened, she found herself squeezed into the front seat of the van, with Lyall jammed against her on one side and Goldie on the other.

She edged as close to Goldie as she could, trying to get away from Lyall. 'Where are we going?'

'To the zoo!' Goldie said, clapping her hands under her chin.

'The *zoo*?'

44

Cassy was so surprised that she glanced at Lyall, to see if it could possibly be true. He grinned sideways at her, mockingly, knowing how annoyed and ill at ease she was.

'Of course the zoo,' he said. 'For research.'

'Oh. *Wolves*.'

Lyall gave her another long, sideways look, as if she amused him. Then he turned the wheel sharply as they went round a corner, so that she was flung to the right, against his shoulder.

Cassy grabbed at Goldie to pull herself upright and then slumped down in her seat, glaring at the road ahead.

She didn't believe they were going to do research. That was a solemn, serious thing, and they were like people out on a jaunt. Surely the wolves were just an excuse.

But when they got there, she found that she was wrong.

Lyall drove past the main gates of the zoo and turned down a side entrance that was blocked by a barrier. As he jumped out, to speak to the gatekeeper, Goldie beamed at Cassy.

'He's always so well organized.'

Cassy glowered and said nothing.

The next moment they were in. The barrier went up and Lyall drove into the yard beyond and parked the van. Then he reached over into the back for Cassy's mac.

'You'll need this. It's getting quite windy out there.'

'Thanks,' Cassy said grumpily. She got out and put the mac on, pulling the belt tight round her waist.

By the time she was ready, the other two had started. Lyall was striding across the yard and down the side of the zoo, with Goldie skipping along beside him. *They wouldn't notice if I wasn't there*, Cassy thought. But she didn't know how long they would be, and there seemed to be no point in sitting in the van. She began to follow them, down paths and round corners, taking care to stay about ten metres behind.

Then suddenly she came round a corner and found that they had stopped. They were standing close to some low outer railings, staring into an enclosure that ran along one side of the zoo. Bare brown earth rose to a hillock in the centre. Bare winter trees clustered round, like the ghost of a forest. And, on top of the hillock, huddled four shapes with pricked ears.

The wolves.

Cassy's mind went very still. Last night she had struggled to make that image in her mind. To mould it with her hands. To describe the subtle, unnamed colour of those coats and the elegant shape of those narrow faces. Now she didn't need to struggle any more. The wolves were there, and she knew that there was nothing like them. They were themselves.

As she watched, two more of them padded from the far side of the enclosure, moving lightly on big, pale feet. They were alert, but their slant eyes watched the other wolves, not the people beyond the railings. The ghost forest where they lived was a place of its own, with its own rules.

Lyall beckoned to Cassy. 'Come and talk to Goldie. I have to meet someone.'

As he disappeared round the far corner, Cassy slid along the rail. But Goldie did not seem to notice that she was there. She was gazing at the wolves, with a wide, unblinking stare. They were all on their feet now, padding steadily round the enclosure, and their movements seemed to hypnotize her.

Goldie and the wolves.

Cassy remembered something that had puzzled her the day before. Touching Goldie's arm, to rouse her, she said, 'What made you think of wolves? For the Moongazer show?'

'What?' Goldie turned, blinking.

'You said that you were the one who had the idea for Lyall's new show. But whatever made you think of wolves?'

'I—I just did.'

Goldie glanced all round, nervously, and Cassy stared at her. Wolves. . . wolves. . . Something danced at the back of her mind and this time she was determined to pin it down. Goldie *must* tell her.

'You can't have made it up all by yourself,' she said. 'You don't know anything about wolves, do you?'

Goldie tossed her head. 'I know you think I'm stupid. You and Granny Phelan think I'm an idiot. But I'm not. I know a lot more than you think. Look.'

She pointed, suddenly, at the hillock inside the enclosure. One of the wolves was standing on top of it, tail erect and head in the air.

'See him?' she said solemnly. 'He's the top wolf and he's

telling the others who's boss. That's how wolves talk to each other. By the way they stand and how they hold their heads and tails.'

'Someone told you that,' Cassy said slowly. 'Was it Lyall?'

'*Lyall?* He doesn't know anything about wolves really. Only what he's read in books. He's never stood for days and days watching them, like me and Mick—'

Goldie broke off suddenly and clapped her hand to her mouth.

'Mick?' said Cassy.

The name felt strange in her mouth and perhaps she had never spoken it out loud before. She had always known, ever since she was very small, that it was forbidden. *We won't talk about him now, Cassy. And don't you go asking your mother, either. She knows she's not to tell you. It'll be time enough when you're grown up.*

But, grown up or not, the taboo was broken now. The name hung in the air between them and Cassy said it again, listening to her own voice.

'Mick.' And then, 'Does *he* like wolves?'

'Don't tell Lyall!' Goldie grabbed at Cassy's arm. 'He goes crazy. You saw how he was this morning when you gave Mick's knock.'

'Of course I won't tell him,' Cassy said scornfully. 'But why take the risk? Why did you choose wolves, in the first place?'

Goldie looked down at her feet. 'Because—because it's like—' She grabbed suddenly at Cassy's arm, squeezing it hard. 'Don't you *remember*? Don't you remember coming here with us in your pushchair, to look at the wolves? Before Granny Phelan took you. When Mick—went away.'

'No.' Cassy's voice was cold. 'I don't remember anything before I lived with Nan.'

'We came almost every week,' Goldie said dreamily. 'Just to stand here and stare. You were so sweet, and you loved seeing the wolves. But not as much as Mick did. They would look at him, and he would look at them. On and on and on—'

'Sounds really wild,' Cassy said drily.

'But that's what he's like, you see. He never gives up. He never goes away until he gets what he wants.' Goldie tossed her head and the emerald-green beret bobbed defiantly. 'So later on—when everyone turned against him—*I* understood. It was only like a wolf, fighting for its own territory.'

'*What* territory? For heaven's sake—' Cassy gripped the railings in front of her. 'What happened?'

Goldie tilted her head back and the winter sun glinted on her hair. 'And the way they've never managed to catch him all these years. Not even Special Branch. That's like a wolf, too. One of those lone wolves he was always going on about. Custer Wolf, or the Traveller, or Three Toes of the Devil.'

'But why don't you tell me?' Cassy's heart pounded and all the years of not speaking clogged her tongue. *There's things a child can't understand,* Nan always said. *Never trouble trouble till trouble troubles you.* All her life she had been waiting to find out, but for a second she couldn't put her questions into words.

And then it was too late. While she was still struggling, Goldie turned suddenly, putting a finger to her lips. 'Sssh! He's coming back!'

A strange woman's voice spoke, from somewhere out of sight. ' . . . they get fed three times a week.'

The next moment, Lyall and the woman came round the corner, talking intently. Lyall grinned as he passed Goldie and Cassy, but he didn't say anything. He was too busy listening to the keeper.

' . . . three twenty-pound joints,' she said, 'with supplements of cod liver oil and bonemeal sprinkled on them . . . '

As she spoke, she unhooked a bunch of keys from her belt. When they reached the far end of the enclosure, she bent and unlocked the gate that led through the outer railings.

'What's happening?' muttered Cassy.

'Oh, Lyall *will* be pleased!' Goldie clapped her hands, innocent and delighted, as though she had no secrets. 'He was hoping they would do that.'

'Let him in, you mean?' Cassy stared as Lyall and the keeper walked towards the inner enclosure. 'Is that safe?'

'Of course it's safe,' Goldie said, like a child repeating a lesson. 'Wolves aren't really fierce and horrible. They're brave and clever and they work together.'

This time, Cassy did not ask where the words had come

from. Instead, she turned and watched as Lyall stepped through the second gate and the keeper locked it after them.

The wolves had all turned to stare as the lock clicked. Now, still moving with steady, unhurried paces, they padded to the far fence and stood watching as Lyall and the keeper walked towards the hillock.

As soon as the two of them were clear of the fence, three wolves slunk behind them, covering the way back to the gate. Pacing backwards and forwards, they sniffed carefully at the tracks on the ground, crossing and recrossing them.

Cassy gripped the outer rail. They wouldn't have taken him in there if it weren't safe. Lyall wasn't worried. Goldie wasn't worried. The keeper wasn't worried. But—

She couldn't drive the pictures out of her head. Grey shapes, moving like water under dark trees. . . Tireless feet, padding on and on across the snow. . . Yellow eyes, gleaming beyond the camp fire . . .

Lyall and the keeper were completely ringed by wolves. Six sharp wolf-faces, watching every step. Six wolf-bodies moving constantly to keep their distance and the shape of their circle. As though they had somehow planned it. Cassy knew, with her rational mind, that there was no threat, but that did not silence the primitive voice crying in her head. *Danger! Danger!*

'Mick would be dead jealous if he could see that,' Goldie muttered in her ear. 'He always wanted to go in there.'

Cassy swallowed and turned her back, pushing her hands deep into her mac pockets. The fingers of her left hand picked at a square corner, but her mind was full of wolves. Wolves and fathers and solemn little boys who did not meet your eyes. It took her a moment to realize what she had found. When she did, she pulled it out and frowned.

> *This is a squat. Goldie is living with a man called Lyall and his son Robert . . .*

She had forgotten to post her card to Nan and the message was already out of date. It should have said something quite different. Something like:

> *We are at the zoo. Goldie's boyfriend is in the wolf cage and Goldie is talking about wolves. And my father. I*

didn't know he was interested in wolves. You've never
told me anything about him. And it's time you did.

For a minute she almost grinned. How would Nan look if she got a postcard like that? Angry? Amazed? She certainly wouldn't send back any answers.

Cassy looked down again at the postcard in her hand. At least it had the right address on. It was time she told Nan where to find her. She had better make sure it got posted.

She clutched it firmly, not putting it back in her pocket. There was no postbox in sight, and she couldn't wander off to find one, but she wasn't going to let herself forget again. She was going to make sure that she sent that postcard before she went to bed. It was a signal, that meant, *Here I am. Come and get me*.

By tomorrow, Nan will know where I am, she thought that night. It should have been comforting, to know that the postcard was on its way, but the idea niggled at the back of her mind as she lay down to sleep.

Here I am . . .
Come and get me . . .

There was something wrong, but she couldn't work out what it was.

* * *

. . . it was a dream with no pictures. Everything came to her through other senses.

The sugary freshness of the pine trees was all around, but under that, half-hidden and confusing, was another, wilder smell. Strong and animal.

Her right hand gripped the handle of the basket, feeling its familiar smoothness. But under her left hand was thick hair, springy and strange. It was so deep that she could run her fingers through it.

Those things were very close. Vividly real. The voice was much fainter. Remote and indistinct, so that she heard it rise and fall without catching any of the words.

But because she was in a dream, she knew that it was her own voice. Telling the way. . .

CHAPTER 7

Stupid! Idiotic!—she ought to have KNOWN—now there was danger, danger—

She had to work it out, but she didn't know what she had done—and it was nearly too late.

Danger, danger, DANGER—

For heaven's sake.

Cassy sat up, wrenching her mind out of the dream. Whatever was the matter with her? She never dreamed. Never, never. But she knew, as she sat there with her heart thumping, that she had dreamed every night in that house.

Her mind scrabbled for a way to make sense of it. It must be the hard floor. Perhaps she needed a mattress.

Something dark and unnerving laughed mockingly inside her head. Something that had nothing to do with floors or mattresses. Grey shapes, moving like water under dark trees . . . Tireless feet, padding on and on across the snow . ... Yellow eyes, gleaming beyond the camp fire . . .

Wolves.

Her stomach turned over and she sat up suddenly, shaking her head to clear it. There was a link there, somewhere. The danger and the fear and the wolves . . . if only she could make her brain work!

But the dream slithered away, out of reach already. She pushed back the blankets and stood up. Perhaps work would drive the cobwebs out of her head. Had she got time to finish clearing the kitchen?

She glanced at her watch, blinked—and then stared.

Eleven o'clock?

How could she possibly have slept until eleven o'clock? The watch must be wrong. But it didn't look wrong. The seconds were ticking away at the same steady pace as usual. And when she lifted her head to stare at the window, she could see that the light behind the blanket was strong and bright.

She began to throw on her clothes as fast as she could. Her hands shook and she had a queer, queasy feeling, but she refused to take any notice of that. *No use moaning over last night's mistakes.* That was what Nan said. *You can only start from where you are.* And she was at eleven o'clock in the morning, with nothing done.

By ten past eleven, she was washed and dressed and unbelievably hungry. She pushed open the kitchen door, to hunt for some food and see if Robert was there.

He wasn't. There was no one there. But three dirty plates were stacked on the floor beside the tap and there was a new litter of eggshells and empty tins on top of the rubbish sack. Even Goldie and Lyall must be up.

Cassy put on the kettle and sorted out some bread and honey, moving very briskly, to keep her mind busy. She could hear feet shuffling around upstairs and when her breakfast was ready she climbed the stairs, with a sandwich in one hand and a mug of tea in the other.

'Yes?' Robert said, when she tapped on the door of the front bedroom.

Cassy pushed the door open and saw that he was the only person in the room. He was sitting on the floor surrounded by papier-mâché masks, with the wolf mask in one hand. Frowning at it.

Wolves.

'Hallo,' Cassy said, more sharply than she meant to. 'Why didn't you wake me up?'

'What for?' muttered Robert, not lifting his head.

She sighed. 'Because it's ridiculous to sleep till eleven o'clock. Isn't it?'

'Mmm.' Robert gave her a vague look and went back to staring at the mask.

'You're not listening!'

'Mmm.'

'Robert!'

'What?' Robert looked up at last, with an apologetic grin. 'I'm sorry. I'm trying to work something out.'

'About that?' Cassy stared down at the wolf mask. 'Isn't it nearly finished?'

'That's what *I* thought.' He sounded exasperated. 'It has to go to Earl tomorrow, to be painted in time for Monday.'

'So what's the problem?'

'Lyall's decided—*now*—that the bottom jaw should move. So it can snap its teeth. And there's no time to make a new mask. I'll have to alter this one.'

Cassy looked at the mask. 'Is it really worth the bother?'

'I'm afraid so.' Robert pulled a face. 'Lyall's right, isn't he? It *would* be much better if the wolf could snap. And it's easy enough to cut round the muzzle—here—so the bottom jaw's separate, joined by hinges.'

'So what's the problem?'

Robert held out the wolf mask. For a split second Cassy hesitated, looking at the long, exaggerated muzzle. Then she reached out and took it. Immediately she saw what was worrying him. The muzzle was so long that the whole head tilted forward, off balance.

'See?' Robert said. 'Lyall's going to have trouble managing that as it is. It'll be impossible with extra bits on the front. And how do we stop the bottom jaw flopping open all the time?'

Cassy grinned. Robert's methodical organization was rather daunting. It was nice to find out that he wasn't very practical.

'You need a counter-weight,' she said briskly. 'Something heavy fitted into the back of the head, and the back of the jaw too. Then it will balance, even though the front sticks out much more.'

'Hey, yes!' Robert's frown vanished. 'What can we use?'

'It'll have to be something heavy that we can mould.' Cassy ran her fingers round inside the mask. 'There's not much spare space, in here.'

'Cloth?' Robert said.

'Not heavy enough.'

'Clay?'

'There isn't time. It would have to dry out before the mask could be painted. You haven't got any Plasticine, have you, or something like that?'

Robert shook his head. 'I don't think we—' Then he

grinned. 'What about that yellow stuff of yours? From the bag of food. Was it precious, or could we use that?'

'I—'

Cassy's mouth went dry, for no reason that she could understand. Instinctively, without being able to explain it, she wanted to refuse.

But that was ridiculous.

'Why not?' she said firmly. 'Let's see if it will do.'

The two of them ran downstairs, with Robert in the lead. He pushed open the door of Cassy's room and saw the yellow lump straightaway, on the mantelpiece.

'Looks like you've been playing around with it already. Does it mould OK?'

'Fine,' Cassy said. 'And it's heavy, too. It's just what we want.'

Robert walked across and picked up the lump, weighing it in one hand. As he did so, he glanced at the photograph next to it. 'Who's the little boy?'

'It's—my dad.'

'Looks like you.' Robert leaned closer. 'Is he still around, or did he take off for good, like my mum?'

'He—' Cassy looked down at her feet. 'I've never seen him. Not since I was a baby. And that's the only photo I've got. Nan hasn't got any pictures of him grown up.'

Robert looked sideways at her, thoughtfully. 'None at all? You mean—you wouldn't recognize him if you passed him in the street?'

'No,' Cassy said firmly. She reached across and took the yellow lump out of Robert's hands. 'Shall we go and do this now, or do we have to wait for Lyall?'

'We can't wait for him,' said Robert. 'He and Goldie have gone to do a show in Hackney. They won't be back until about five.'

'Let's get going, then.'

Cassy led the way. She had had enough of vague feelings and unanswerable questions. What she wanted was a straight-forward, practical job. Like altering the mask. Before Robert even reached the front bedroom, she had picked up a Stanley knife.

'Want me to cut out this bottom jaw?'

55

Robert hesitated. 'It might be tricky. And we're sunk if you wreck the mask.'

'I won't wreck it.' Confidently Cassy began to mark out a jagged line on the papier-mâché muzzle. 'We'll have it all done before Lyall and Goldie get back.'

'Brilliant. They won't want to be fussing with the masks when they've finished a show.'

Cassy scored two long fangs at the front of the wolf's head. 'What show are they doing?'

'One of the old ones.' Throwing back his head, Robert declaimed in a fair imitation of Lyall's voice: 'The Daring and Terrible Tale of the Great Conquest of Peru'. Then he grinned. 'Schools ask for that one a lot. They all start off making breast-plates and feathers, and they end up taking sides and having furious arguments.'

'Sounds good. Why are we fussing with all this wolf stuff when he's got a show like that?'

'What d'you mean?'

'Well!' Cassy snorted and waved a hand at the masks lying all over the floor. 'The Wolf and The Three Little Pigs! Who's going to want that when they can have the Conquest of Peru?'

'But that's only a little bit of it!' Robert stared as if she were feeble-minded. 'You've seen all the stuff in my file. Pictures, facts, ideas. The thing's *enormous*.'

Cassy reached for the wire-cutters. 'But wolves are only animals.'

'You still think that?' Robert looked at her for a moment, but he didn't say anything. Picking up the yellow lump, he began to mould it into a longer, thinner shape. 'What do we want? A sausage to go at the back of the neck?'

Cassy nodded. 'And two bits left over, for the sides of the jaw. Now shut up. I want to concentrate while I cut.'

And, with a steady hand, she sliced into the wolf's head.

It took her almost half an hour to cut all the way round the muzzle, shaping the fangs as she went. As the last inch parted, Robert gave an approving nod. 'You're pretty good at things like that, aren't you?'

'That's because of Nan.' Cassy grinned. '*No point in having a clever head if you've got stupid hands*, she says.'

Robert raised an eyebrow and looked thoughtfully at her. 'The terrifying Granny Phelan?'

'She's not terrifying,' Cassy said quickly.

'She terrifies Goldie. You should hear the things *she* says about your precious Nan.'

'Well I don't know what would have happened to Goldie if Nan wasn't around,' Cassy said indignantly. 'Whenever she gets into a real muddle, Nan comes and sorts her out. What else does she want?'

'How about—you?' Robert stopped smiling and looked hard at Cassy. 'She'd like you to live with her all the time, you know. She hated it when Granny Phelan stole you away.'

'But she had to!' Cassy said fiercely. She'd worked that one out years ago. 'She *couldn't* have left me with Goldie. Not once—'

'Once your dad went off?' Robert said softly. 'Yes, what *was* all that about?'

Cassy felt her face turn stiff and obstinate. 'Why should it be about anything?'

'Because—oh, I don't know.' Robert shrugged. 'Look at the way Goldie shuts up about him. She jabbers on about everything else under the sun, but ask her a question about Marvellous Mick and—nothing. Utter silence. And you looked odd, too, when I was asking you those questions downstairs.'

'What do you mean *odd*?'

It took Robert a moment to work out the right words. 'You looked . . . out of your depth. As if you didn't know what you were talking about.' He hesitated, and then went on. 'You looked frightened.'

'*Frightened?*' Cassy gave a squawk of laughter that was just too loud. 'How can I be frightened? I don't know a thing about him.'

She could tell from Robert's face that he didn't believe her. 'Oh come on. You must know *something*. Your Nan must have told you about him.'

'Why?' Cassy glared at him, defiantly. 'Why should anyone tell me about him? He's gone.'

'But—you need to know. He's your father, for heaven's sake. I *made* Lyall tell me all about my mother.'

'You can't *make* Nan do anything,' Cassy said stiffly. 'She's not like that.'

'Aha! So she *is* terrifying!'

It was only a joke. But Cassy didn't want jokes about Nan. She didn't want to talk about any of it, any more. Briskly, she picked up the long yellow sausage that Robert had made and began to fit it into the mask, at the back of the neck.

'We need some more papier mâché,' she muttered. 'Strips, to stick over this, to keep it in place.'

To her relief, Robert nodded and began to concentrate on the mask again. A few minutes later, both of them were sticking pieces of paper over the bright yellow shapes inside the wolf's head. Gradually covering them all, until not a scrap of yellow could be seen.

CHAPTER 8

By the time the mask was finished and put to dry, it was well after lunch time.

'What we need after all that work,' Robert said, 'is a good old fry-up. And don't you *dare* tell me that Granny Phelan doesn't approve of fried food.'

'We-ell, she *is* a nurse,' Cassy began solemnly. 'And fried food is amazingly bad for people.'

Robert pulled a rude face and ran down the stairs. By the time Cassy reached the kitchen, he had already got the stove going, and was slitting open a pack of bacon.

'Help me get this ready,' he said, 'and when we've eaten it I'll give you a hand with this kitchen clearing you're so dotty about.'

Cassy grinned and began to look for the bread.

It was almost four o'clock before they got to work. It only took an hour or so to carry out the rest of the broken wood, but when they had finished the kitchen floor was covered with dust and splinters. And before they could begin on that, there was a wild, joyful noise from outside. Someone was driving up the road, banging repeatedly on a car hooter.

Robert dropped the cloth he was holding and ran to open the door. 'That's Lyall and Goldie,' he called over his shoulder. 'The show must have gone really well. I think we're going to have a great evening!'

Lyall and Goldie were like children after a party. They came dancing into the house, grinning all over their faces.

'They cried!' shouted Goldie. 'They cried and argued and lost their tempers—and Lyall said I was wonderful!'

'You're a beautiful golden Inca! A daughter of the Sun!'

Lyall put down the box of paper feathers he was carrying and picked her up in his arms, to whirl her round the hall.

Cassy stood safely out of the way, in the shelter of the kitchen door, and Robert shook his head at them. 'Never mind about being wonderful. Did you get the cheque?'

'Of course we did, dear business manager!' Lyall put Goldie down and hunted through the pockets of his jeans. 'Ah! Here we are. A hundred pounds plus expenses.'

Cassy gasped out loud, before she could stop herself. All that? For a day spent playing around? It didn't seem right to her, but Robert took the crumpled cheque as if it were the most ordinary thing in the world. Smoothing it out carefully, he copied the figure into a notebook before he put the cheque away in his wallet.

Then he glanced down the hall at Cassy. 'Coming to help me empty the van?'

'If you like.' She edged past Lyall and Goldie, who were dancing in circles, and followed Robert out of the house. 'What's the matter with them?' she hissed when they reached the van. 'Have they been drinking?'

'Of course not.' Robert lifted out a huge golden disc and pushed it into her arms. 'They're just on a high, that's all. From doing the show.'

'I thought it was supposed to be *work*,' Cassy muttered disapprovingly.

'It is.' Turning round from the van, Robert gave her a long, puzzled look. 'What's that got to do with anything?'

'Well, they just look as though they've been having fun.'

'They have. *I* have fun when *I* work. And I bet you do, too. You really enjoyed clearing out that kitchen, didn't you?'

'Of course not!'

'Why do it then?' Robert lifted out two boxes and shut the van. 'What was the point if you didn't enjoy it?'

Cassy wondered whether he was teasing her, but he didn't seem to be. 'It *had* to be done.'

'Why?'

'Because you can't live like that.'

'Why not?'

'Because—because—' How could you talk to someone with no proper ideas about anything? 'Nan always says—'

'I don't want to know what *she* says.' Robert slammed the van doors and locked them. 'I want to know why you agree with her.'

'Because—'

Cassy didn't know how she was going to end the sentence and she never found out. Before she could get any further, Lyall came bounding down the path and grabbed the golden disc.

'Stop fussing with those things, you two. I want FOOD!'

'We've got sausages,' Robert began. 'And—'

Lyall grinned and growled at him, baring his teeth. 'I'm sick of sausages. Don't be so bloody economical, Robert! We did three shows last week and we've got four next week, besides the one on Friday. We can afford something better than sausages.'

His eyes brightened and he lurched towards Cassy, arms outstretched.

'Juicy meat! Sugar and spice! Curried Cassy!'

Cassy stepped back, away from his long, crooked fingers and his red, open mouth with its rows of teeth. But that only made matters worse. Lyall lurched closer, with a wicked leer.

'No escape! No escape! Unless you have a silver bullet to shoot me with. And even then, no power will free your flesh from my FANGS!'

How could he? In the *street*! Cassy stepped sideways, into the shelter of the van, and glared at his mocking, contorted face. Hating him.

'Knock it off, Lyall,' Robert said calmly. 'You can see she doesn't like it. Do you want me to go out and get a curry?'

Lyall grinned and growled again, still wolfish. 'Hot! And *now*!'

'Now?' Robert looked at his watch. 'Oh, I suppose that place in Steelyard Lane might be open. OK, I'll go.'

'I'll come too,' Cassy said hastily. She didn't want to be left alone with Lyall and Goldie. 'Wait while I get my coat.'

It was when they were coming back that they saw the man. As they hurried round the corner of Albert Street, carrying warm, heavy paper bags, Robert suddenly laid a hand on Cassy's arms. 'Look.'

'What?'

He put a finger to his lips and nodded down towards the Moongazer van, pulling Cassy into the shadow of a hedge. Then he whispered, with his lips right up to her ear. 'We've had trouble with the van before. Looks like they're back again.'

The street was already dark and it took Cassy a moment or two to make out the dark shape. He was round behind the van, on the road side, a crouched figure in a tracksuit, with the hood pulled up close round his head.

'I don't think he's fiddling with it,' she muttered back at Robert. 'He's tying up his shoelace or something, isn't he?'

'Ssh!' Robert laid his hand lightly over her mouth and the two of them peered round the hedge, straining their eyes to see what the man was doing.

For several moments, he did not move at all. Then, just as Cassy was losing patience, he darted. He glanced up and down the empty street and then ran forward into the alley at the side of their house.

'Come on!' said Robert. He was away down the road before Cassy had taken in what he meant. By the time she caught up with him, he was coming back out of the alley, shaking his head.

'Too late. He must have got over the wall at the back.'

'But what? Who—?'

Robert shrugged. 'Someone from the owners I expect.'

'The owners?'

'Of the house, of course. Trying to get us out.' He said it quite casually, as though it were a normal thing. 'Owners always want you out, even if they're only waiting to knock the house down.'

'But I thought they had to take you to court.'

'That's too slow for some of them. And not—personal enough.' Robert narrowed his eyes, but Cassy did not want to know what he was remembering.

'What are you going to do about it?' she said quickly.

'Not a lot we can do. Only tell Lyall.'

But Lyall wasn't interested in their intruder. They both

started to explain at once, as soon as he opened the door, but he refused to be serious about it.

'You didn't see his face? Are you sure it wasn't grey and hairy under the mask? Perhaps there were long pointed teeth, snapped together like a trap. And . . .'

'Oh don't be silly,' said Cassy.

But Lyall didn't take any notice. 'The ligahooooo,' he whispered, drawing out the last syllable like a distant howl. 'With his great mouth gaping and his silent, shadowless feet. How can you be sure . . . ?'

Robert grinned, but Cassy was in no mood for games.

'I don't believe in ghosts!' she snapped.

'Nothing ghostly about the ligahoo.' Lyall gave her a wide, angelic smile and lifted the bag of curry out of her hands. 'It chases you with real feet. And bites you with real, sharp TEETH!'

Still grinning, he padded past Cassy and made for the stairs. Robert went after him, so that Cassy had no choice but to follow, if she wanted her dinner.

The candles were lit again in the mirror room, for the first time since her arrival. And there, in the magic forest, sat Goldie, cross-legged on the mattress. She wore a purple and gold muslin skirt draped over her knees and down to her ankles, and her hair hung down her back in a single, thick braid.

She smiled dreamily as the others came in. 'Let's eat now. I'm starving.'

'The feast is prepared,' said Lyall. Putting down the bag he was carrying, he began to lift the cartons out on to the floorboards.

Cassy glanced round. 'I'll go and get the plates and the cutlery.'

'No more school dinners!' Lyall pulled a face, spreading his hands wide with distaste. 'Goldie and I have suffered one today and that's enough. Now we will have a magic feast, to take away the taste of cabbage.'

'But how are we going to eat it without plates?' Cassy said.

Robert put his bag down beside Lyall's. 'Out of the cartons, of course. With our fingers and the chapattis.'

'Eat with our *fingers?*' Cassy was horrified. 'But that's—'

'Wild?' Lyall said mockingly. 'Savage?' Very lightly, he

flicked the tip of her nose, with one thumb. 'What's the matter, Cassy? Will civilization be destroyed if we don't use a knife and fork? Shall we drop down on to all fours and tear the food with our teeth?'

Goldie went into peals of laughter, but Robert looked sympathetically at Cassy.

'It's just another way of eating, you know. You don't grab handfuls. You use the thumb and the first two fingers of your right hand, very delicately. Look.'

Opening a carton, he demonstrated for her, neatly scooping rice in his crooked fingers. And grudgingly, Cassy saw that it wasn't uncivilized. It was even elegant, in a strange, alien way. But she knew that she could never eat like that herself.

'I'm going to get myself a plate,' she said stiffly. 'And a knife and fork. Does anyone else want one?'

There was no answer, except a grin from Lyall. Cassy marched out of the room and down to the kitchen, feeling her way in the shadows. The dirty plates from the morning were still heaped by the tap, covered in wood dust now, as well as tomato sauce. She washed one, angrily, and rummaged in the box of cutlery for a knife and fork. She was even angrier by the time she began to climb the stairs again.

Lyall's voice met her half-way. Not his ordinary speaking voice, but something richer and darker and deeper. Even before she could make out the words, it sent a long, fascinated shiver across the back of her shoulders. And then, as she reached the last few steps, she heard what he was saying.

' " . . . and you must do it at the next full moon," said the wise woman. "For it is *bzou*, the werewolf, who troubles your sleep and he cannot be destroyed, except by this silver bullet." '

Cassy hesitated for a moment, her hand on the stair rail. What was going on *now*?

' "But be warned!" ' Lyall's voice was sharper now, every word distinct. ' "You must not speak of this—not even to your dear father. If you do, the bullet will lose its power and there will be nothing to save you." '

Creeping up the last few stairs, Cassy moved carefully into

the room and sat down beside Goldie. Lyall's voice did not waver, and neither of the others looked round as she scooped food on to her plate. Goldie was sitting spellbound, her hand half-way to her mouth, and Robert was rolling a piece of chapatti in his fingers as he stared at Lyall.

'The girl thanked her and went home,' Lyall continued. 'She hid the gun and the silver bullet under her pillow and spoke of them to no one. Not even to her father. But at the next full moon . . . '

He paused, not teasing, but drawing them into the story. Slowly Cassy put down her fork, watching his eyes.

'At the next full moon,' he murmured, 'she was woken by soft, heavy footsteps under her window. They padded to the door, and there was a muffled tap, low down. Two taps, and then a pause, and then two more . . . '

Cassy's breath caught suddenly in her throat and time stopped, so that the words went on and on repeating themselves in her head. *Two taps, and then a pause, and then two more . . .* She forgot the warm plate on her knees and the tangle of flames and mirrors all around her. All she could see was the picture that leapt into her mind.

The hand lifted to tap twice and then twice again. Tapping on the spotless, blue-painted door that she knew better than any door in the world.

The door of Nan's flat.

Now she knew where she had heard that signal. She knew why it had come so easily to her hand the day before. She knew—a hundred things that exploded suddenly in her head, like the answers to questions she had never wanted to ask.

'For an instant,' murmured Lyall, still telling his story, 'she saw the terrible face at the window. The grey muzzle, the pricked ears and the long, murderous fangs. Shaking with terror, she pulled the pistol from under her pillow—and fired!'

'And then?' breathed Goldie.

Lyall's voice was soft now, every syllable crystal-clear. 'Then she opened the door and a body slumped across her feet. It was the body of her father, with a bullet hole in his left temple.'

Cassy picked up a chapatti, with trembling hands, and ripped it in half.

* * *

. . . faster, faster! Now she was alone, hurrying through the forest on a narrow, twisting path. The basket dragged at her arm and she had to stop and catch her breath, but there was no time to rest properly. Faster!

The path twisted and twisted again. At every turn she looked for a hint of smoke ahead, or a glimpse of the white cottage wall. But there was nothing. Only more trees and longer shadows and another twist of the path. On and on she ran, stumbling and sliding on the rough mossy track. Surely the cottage would be round the next turn.

Or the next.

Or the next . . .

CHAPTER 9

She woke to a clatter and a crash and the sound of loud, angry voices. Upstairs, Goldie was screaming. Shrieking and swearing so loudly that her voice cracked in her throat.

' . . . bloody get out of here! Fall off the roof! Crack your goddam fascist *skull!*'

Lyall was yelling too, not hysterically, but in a loud, firm voice. 'This is our home! Do you hear that? We don't allow you to come in! You're committing a criminal offence!'

There were feet running from the front bedroom to the back and somewhere higher up, outside, there was a slithering, scraping sound and the crash of slates falling from the roof.

Cassy was on her feet within a minute. She grabbed her mac round her and headed for the stairs, stumbling against the bottom step in the darkness. Before she was half-way up, two figures came flying down, in the opposite direction. Lyall and Robert. They leaped past her.

'See to Goldie,' Lyall yelled as Cassy flattened herself against the wall. 'Keep her inside.'

The next moment they had gone, banging the front door behind them. Cassy heard their feet racing along the pavement towards the side alley. Running upstairs, into the mirror room, she found Goldie standing at the window, banging her hand against the frame.

'Get out, get out, get *out!*' she was yelling. 'Go away! Leave us alone!'

As Cassy came up behind her, she saw Lyall and Robert burst out of the alley and into the garden. Lyall threw himself at the line of bushes along the fence, thumping and shaking them as he ran down the garden. Robert stood on the grass, waiting.

'What's going on?' said Cassy.

'They're out there!' Goldie hissed, gripping the window

frame. 'We heard them drop down, but we didn't see them run. They must be in the bushes.' She banged her hand hard on the glass and yelled again, fiercely, 'Get them, Lyall! Don't let them get away! Show them they can't just put us out!'

'But who are they?'

'They—oh look!'

Lyall was nearly at the bottom of the garden. Suddenly, just ahead of him, a dark shape had jumped out from behind Cassy's pile of broken wood.

'It's him!' Cassy shouted.

The man she and Robert had seen. He was unmistakable. The tracksuit hood was still pulled up close round his head, and he ran with a strange, stooping gait, awkward-looking, but very fast. No one who had ever seen that could fail to recognize it.

He was agile as well as fast. The moment Lyall and Robert saw him, they charged, but the man was on top of the wall before they could reach him. He went up like a lizard, as though his hands and feet knew all the holds, and then swung over in one swift movement.

Cassy heard Goldie gasp, sharply, but she did not take any notice. She was too busy watching that quick, dark figure. Lyall and Robert had no chance of catching him. For a second, they scrabbled at the wall, but they couldn't find the handholds in the dark. After a couple of seconds, they gave up and began to walk round the garden, checking all the other hiding-places.

'Well, at least they've got rid of *him*,' Cassy said. 'But there were some more, weren't there?'

'No,' Goldie said. Very softly. 'There won't be anyone else.'

Cassy did look at her then. Because she had changed completely. A moment before, she had been like a demon, thundering on the window and shrieking into the garden. Now she was standing very still, staring down.

'What's the matter?' Cassy said. 'Are you all right?'

'I—yes, of course I am.' Goldie took a step backwards, swayed slightly and grabbed at Cassy's shoulder to stop herself falling.

Her voice was expressionless and her eyes were wide and unblinking. *Shock*. Cassy seized on the idea because it gave her something useful to do. She put her arm round Goldie's waist and steered her across the room, towards the mattress.

'Sit down for a bit, until you feel all right. We're quite safe here.'

Goldie slumped down on to the mattress and sat with her head on her knees and her hair falling in a great cascade all round her, looking shrunken and miserable.

'What happened?' Cassy said. 'Was he up on the roof? How did you know he was there?'

'He set off the booby trap,' Goldie said, in the same dull, faint voice. 'Didn't you hear all the things falling down? He was on the roof, trying to get in through the skylight. He was—'

She stopped.

'But what was he doing? Was he a burglar? Or someone trying to get you out of the house?'

Goldie lifted her head. 'But I thought you recognized him.'

'Recognized him?'

'You said "It's him!" I heard you.'

She was staring at Cassy with big, round eyes, as though she expected something special. But Cassy was baffled. 'Robert and I saw him yesterday, watching the house. But I don't know who he is.'

'He was here yesterday, as well?' Goldie whispered. 'I didn't know.'

'Perhaps Lyall didn't want to upset you.'

'Upset me? Why should I be *upset*?'

Cassy began to feel impatient. 'Oh well, it doesn't matter, does it? He's gone now.'

'He never goes,' Goldie muttered. 'Not until he's got what he wants.'

There was something wrong with that. Something out of place. But before Cassy could work out what it was, Lyall and Robert were knocking at the front door.

She ran down to let them in and found Lyall fuming on the doorstep.

'Missed him! Did you see? If I'd only had the wit to start at the other end of the garden, we could have grabbed him and found out who he was working for.'

'*Must* have been the owners,' Robert said. 'It was just like that time at Wandsworth when the heavies came in. Remember? When Earl slid in the butter and let them go, and Goldie went berserk.'

'Like a tiger.' Lyall grinned, calming down. 'I bet you had to hold her back when he went over the wall, Cassy!'

'Well—'

Cassy hesitated and his grin vanished. 'What's the matter? Is there something wrong with her?'

'She—no, I think she's OK,' Cassy said slowly. 'She went very quiet when she saw the man and now she's rather—peculiar. I think she must be suffering from shock.'

Lyall glanced at Robert. 'I'll go and see her. You go up to the roof and reset the booby trap.'

Then he was off, taking the stairs at a run. Cassy shook her head.

'He's always fussing over Goldie. And that just makes her worse.'

'I think he's worried,' Robert said drily. 'It's not like Goldie to cave in. We usually have problems keeping her out of the fight.'

'So? Perhaps she got frightened this time. With it all happening so suddenly, in the dark.'

'There's nothing to be frightened about,' Robert said. 'They can't put us out without a possession order.'

'But you haven't got a right to be here, have you?'

'Goldie had a *right* to be in that dump your precious Nan found her,' Robert said coldly. 'But she was frightened all the time there. She's no good at living on her own. If your Nan really cared, she wouldn't have left her there.'

'But we couldn't—'

'Look, why don't you just go back to bed and forget the whole thing? I've got to do the booby trap, but there's no call for you to miss any more sleep.'

He strode off up the hall and Cassy glared after him. Stupid, pompous idiot! What did he know about—about anything? Nan had struggled to look after Goldie. She'd found her a room. Shown her how to keep it clean. Told her how to spend her money to make it go round. Done *everything* for her.

Except take her in.

But that was ridiculous! Cassy pushed the thought away and

70

stamped into her bedroom. Why should Nan take Goldie in? She wasn't her daughter. Only her daughter-in-law. If she lived with them, the flat would be a squash. And she would drive Nan mad.

And there wouldn't be anywhere to send Cassy, when Nan wanted to get rid of her.

The thought slid into her mind and lodged there, like a sliver of ice. She had never thought of it like that before—but she realized, now, that she had always known. All these visits to Goldie were nothing to do with keeping in touch with her mother. They weren't for Cassy's benefit at all. Nan sent her to Goldie's to get her out of the way of something.

Or someone.

Pulling off her mac, Cassy crawled into the blankets and curled into her usual position. But her brain was humming and she didn't fall asleep.

At three o'clock she was still lying there, wide awake, thinking about Nan and Goldie. Wondering why she hadn't asked questions herself, instead of waiting for Robert to push them at her. Trying not to think about the worst question of all.

Did Nan really want her, or was she just a nuisance?

It all went round and round in her head, growing more muddled and tangled the more she tried to think about it. On and on and on—

It was almost a relief when she heard the noises.

At first there were only a few creaks from the stairs. The sort of sounds any old house might make on its own. If Cassy hadn't been lying awake in the dark, hunting for distractions, she wouldn't even have noticed them.

But, because she noticed them, she listened harder and after a moment she heard another sound. It was the faint noise of bare feet walking down the hall, sticking slightly on the tiles.

Her heart thudded once, twice, and the blood pounded in her ears, drowning out the noise of the footsteps. By the time her head cleared, they were past the door of her room and there was a different sound.

Someone was sliding back the bolts on the front door, very slowly and carefully.

Pushing the blankets away, Cassy sat up. She was afraid to move, so she stared at the window instead. The blanket that Robert had hung there didn't cover it completely, and if she leaned sideways, she could see round the edge and glimpse the end of the garden path.

The front door opened, very, very slowly. Cassy felt the cold air slide into her room and creep across the boards. Then a shadow tiptoed down the path and along the pavement in front of the house, so quickly that she almost missed it.

It was Goldie.

She was wearing her long, pale nightdress, with a shawl over her shoulders, and her hair fell down her back in a tangle. For a second, Cassy wondered whether she were sleepwalking—but she seemed too purposeful for that.

So where was she going?

Cassy stood up, grabbed her mac and her shoes and headed for the front door. Whatever Goldie was doing, it must be stupid. She couldn't be allowed to roam round the streets in her nightdress.

The front door was ajar. Cassy slipped through the gap and tiptoed down the path, but there was no sign of Goldie in the street. The pavements were completely empty, in both directions. She must have gone down the alley.

Running along the short stretch of pavement, Cassy turned down the narrow passage way and began to tiptoe again. She didn't want anyone to see her until she knew what was going on.

As she came out into the garden, she saw Goldie at the far end, standing in front of the wall. Her head was flung back as she gazed up at the spot where the hooded man had flung himself over.

Cassy began to creep closer, padding silently through the long, wet grass. At first she could hear nothing except the traffic in the distance, but when she was about twenty metres away, Goldie whistled.

It wasn't a tune. It was just a quick pattern of notes, in a rhythm that was much too familiar to Cassy by now.

Two short, quick whistles. Then a pause. Then two more.

Cassy froze. She could see how hard Goldie was listening for an answer. Her whole body strained upwards, gleaming silver-gilt in the moonlight, from the crown of her head to the hem of her nightdress. Waiting.

Cassy found that she was waiting, too. It seemed as though there must be a reply, just because Goldie was listening so hard. At any moment a dark, agile shape would swing over the wall and jump down on to the wet grass. His hands would go up to his hood, and he would push it away from his face . . .

But there was no answer.

Goldie waited for more than a minute and then she called, in a low, tense voice. 'Are you there? It's me. Goldie.'

That broke the spell. The dark figure vanished from Cassy's mind, and Goldie seemed ridiculous again. Whatever were the two of them doing, standing in the garden, in the damp grass, when they should have been asleep?

'What's the matter?' Cassy said out loud. 'Why aren't you in bed?'

She should have known better. Goldie turned round, saw her, and screamed.

It wasn't a very loud scream, but it was enough to wake Lyall. The back window rattled up and he bellowed down into the garden.

'Goldie? Cassy? What's the matter?'

Goldie went rigid. Her face was quite clear in the moonlight, and Cassy saw the eyes widen, desperately. She knew that look. Goldie didn't want to say what she had been doing, but she couldn't think of anything else. Her mind was paralysed.

Automatically, without wondering why she did it, Cassy covered for her. Flinging her head back, she called up to Lyall, as casually as she could. 'Sorry. Did we wake you? We just came out to look at the stars.' It was the best she could do, but it sounded weak and unconvincing.

Lyall just barked, 'Come back inside!' and closed the window.

Now there would be a row with him, on top of everything else! Grabbing Goldie's arm, Cassy dragged her up the garden, muttering at her.

'See what you've done? That's what comes of creeping round in the middle of the night. What shall we do if he throws us out of this house? Where shall we go?'

Goldie began to cry quietly, but Cassy hardened her heart. If there was going to be a quarrel with Lyall, she had to key herself up to it. She wouldn't stand there meekly while he bawled her out, even if Goldie did. And she wasn't going to give any explanations, either. Lyall had nothing to do with her.

He was waiting in the doorway when they reached the front of the house, and when he saw them, he scowled.

'What's the point of having booby traps if you go out and leave the door wide open? Haven't you got any sense?'

Goldie grabbed at Cassy's arm. 'The stars!' she gabbled. 'They're so pretty, Lyall. And I really wanted to see the full moon.'

'The full moon's not until Monday!' But the sharpness had gone out of Lyall's voice. He came down the path and put an arm round Goldie's shoulders. 'It's not a good night for stars. Go back to bed, Goldie.'

She glanced up and down the road and then nodded and ran for the stairs. Cassy and Lyall stood side by side, listening to her bare feet slap against the tiles.

'I think she may have been sleepwalking,' said Cassy.

Lyall looked at her. 'No you don't. You know what she was doing, just as well as I do.'

Crying wolf. Crying Mick. Cassy closed her eyes for a second and then walked quickly into the house, with Lyall behind her. They could see Goldie turning the corner at the top of the stairs, almost hidden by the shadows. Lyall pulled the door shut with a thud.

'I bet you think I'm a bloody fool.'

The bitterness in his voice shocked Cassy into answering. 'Why?'

'Living with a woman who sees another man behind every bush.' Lyall gave a sharp, unlovely snort of laughter. 'It's more than twelve years, you know, since she really saw him.'

'But he—'

But he was here tonight. Was it true, or was it just a notion of Goldie's? Before Cassy could make up her mind, Lyall pulled a harsh, sarcastic face.

'And what a man! Perhaps we ought to have his picture hung on our wall, to inspire us! A *real* hero—' His voice caught in his throat and he turned away towards the stairs. But

Cassy could just hear the last few words he muttered, to himself. '—Michael Phelan, the Cray Hill bomber.'

Her ears rang as though he had boxed them. For a second the words were all round her, tingling in the air.

The Cray Hill bomber.

All the questions that had swirled round in her head suddenly came together, clustering round those four words. And a pit of chaos and terror yawned at Cassy's feet.

Michael Phelan—

But in that terrifying instant, Nan's voice was in her head, like rope pulling her to safety.

You don't want to take any notice of Goldie. She's always telling fairy stories. That was it. That had to be the explanation. And everyone knew that fairy stories weren't true.

'Don't be silly,' she said to Lyall's retreating back. 'You can't believe everything that Goldie says.'

Then she marched into her room and shut the door, without looking behind her. But the pieces had slotted together in her head, and she couldn't disconnect them. It was all beginning to make terrible sense.

CHAPTER 10

She was still groggy with it in the morning. Exhausted by thinking *What if . . . ?* and *If it's true that . . .* and *If Goldie's right . . .* It was a relief when Lyall packed her off to the library, to help Robert with his research.

Facts. They were what she wanted. No feelings, no fairy-tales. She sat at the table in the reference library, next to Robert, and wrote down comforting, definite facts, one after another.

INTERNAL PARASITES OF THE WOLF:
9 species of fluke
21 species of tapeworm
24 species of roundworm
3 species of thorny-headed worm, as follows:

That was what wolves were. Animals that lived in the zoo, behind bars, padding on bare earth. They had flukes and roundworms. Tapeworms and thorny-headed worms. They weren't romantic or heroic. And no human being could be like a wolf.

Cassy copied out the long, complicated Latin names, concentrating on each letter, to make certain she got them right. Glad to concentrate, because that stopped her thinking about—other things.

Diphyllobothrium latum
Dipylidium caninum
Echinococcus granulosus . . .

But it was impossible to concentrate like that all the time. Her eyes grew tired and her brain shied away, treacherously, from the safety of tapeworms. Other things began to echo, insistently, at the back of her mind. *Michael Phelan, the Cray*

Hill bomber . . . the yellow stuff from Nan's shopping bag . . .
Mick Phelan . . . bombs . . .

She shook her head fiercely and leaned sideways to see what Robert was doing. He was writing very fast, with such angry energy that his pen cut into the paper. And as he wrote, he muttered under his breath.

'What's up?' Cassy nudged him. 'You're talking to yourself.'

Robert frowned and pushed his notebook across to her. 'Look at *that*.'

It was a page of notes that began in his usual neat writing.

Lost sub-species

Gradually, as he had gone down the page, the words had grown bigger and bigger. English and Latin were mixed together, straggling furiously from side to side, with jagged angry capitals at the end of each line.

Canis lupus beothecus	*Newfoundland wolf*	*EXTINCT*
Canis lupus fuscus	*Cascade Mountains wolf*	*EXTINCT*
Canis lupus irremotus	*N. Rocky Mountains wolf*	*EXTINCT*
Canis lupus mogollensis	*Mogollon Mountain wolf*	*EXTINCT*

Robert stabbed his finger at the words. 'Imagine it! All those have gone. Pouf! We wouldn't leave them the space they needed and now no one will ever see them again.'

Cassy ducked away from his fury and looked down primly at the list.

'It is a pity, isn't it?' she said.

'*A pity*? Don't you realize we're talking about death? Massive, huge deaths of whole groups. Look at this.'

She didn't want to think about that. She wanted to think about little things like tapeworms and liver fluke and roundworms. Ordinary everyday miseries. But Robert was pushing a book under her nose and she couldn't escape from the photograph without making a scene. So she looked.

There was a deer lying in the foreground. And behind it, in

grotesque, twisted positions, sat thirty or forty wolves, arranged in rows.

'All dead!' Robert hissed in her ear. 'Poisoned by a deerful of strychnine. And look at this!' He reached for his notebook and flicked the pages over. 'That's what people do to wolves!'

The list was so long that he had written it in two columns.

traps	*ring hunts*
pits	*drives*
corrals	*hamstringing and lassoing*
deadfalls	*use of dogs*
the ice-box trap	*stalking*
the edge trap	*den hunting*
piercers	*professional hunting*
fishhooks	*bountying*
snares	*poisoning*
set guns	*aerial shooting (with rifles, from*
steel traps	*planes and helicopters)*

Death and violence. Twenty-one ways to kill and maim and destroy.

Facts.

Cassy pushed the notebook away. 'There's no need to get so worked up about it,' she said coldly. 'It's not happening here, is it? Real life's not like that.'

'Real life?' Robert drew back and looked at her. 'What's *real life*?'

'You know as well as I do. Ordinary things—like us sitting here in the library writing. And school and shopping and cleaning.'

Robert raised an eyebrow. 'And nice fitted kitchens? Fathers who go out to work and mothers who stay at home and do the cooking? Electric lights that turn on, and rooms without broken mirrors on the walls?'

'Well—'

'Is our house really part of *real life*?'

'Of course it is!' snapped Cassy. 'Don't be silly. You know what I mean.'

'Do I?' Robert stared thoughtfully at her. 'Would it go on being real life if . . . ' he stopped for a moment, hunting for the right example and then finished triumphantly, ' . . . if a gang of terrorists walked in and took us hostage?'

'Shut up!' Cassy said fiercely. She grabbed her notebook and began to write again as fast as she could.

> *EXTERNAL PARASITES OF THE WOLF:*
> *2 species of lice*
> *1 species of flea*
> *7 species of tick*
> *1 species of tongue worm*
> *1 species of mange mite, as follows:*

But the facts didn't work any more. The question was out in the open now, filling her brain. It pounded away behind everything she read and everything she wrote.

By the end of the day she was exhausted with fighting it. Twenty times the words were on the tip of her tongue.

Robert, do you know what colour plastic explosive is?

But it was stupid to ask him. He wouldn't know the answer—and he would wonder why she had asked.

Over and over again she peered round at the library shelves. There must be a book there, somewhere, that would tell her what she wanted to know. But she hadn't got a clue where to begin, and she could just imagine the librarian's face if she asked.

Why does a girl like you want to know about plastic explosive . . .

She had to keep the whole thing to herself, until she could make up her mind, but the strain was almost unbearable.

As she and Robert walked home that evening, she could hardly take in what he was saying. He was describing the big map he meant them to make that evening, to show where wolves still lived. Cassy nodded and smiled and tried to look intelligent, but she could see him looking at her strangely.

'What's up?' he asked at last. 'Been working too hard? I'm so used to taking notes I forget what hard work it is.'

'Oh. Yes.' Cassy blinked. 'No, it's not that.'

'What is it, then?'

'I—' She still dared not ask the real question, but she edged as close to it as she could. 'I was wondering about that wolf-mask we made. Is it OK? I mean, is the papier mâché dry yet?'

For a second her mind raced. Suppose she bought some Plasticine. Perhaps she could undo the papier mâché—take out the yellow stuff—put in the Plasticine—mend the mask—and then, and then—

'It's fine,' Robert said airily. 'Lyall said he was going to take it up to Wandsworth this afternoon. So that Earl can get it painted in time for Monday.'

'Oh.'

She didn't know if she were relieved or disappointed. Her heart gave a great, breath-taking thump and she gripped her notebook tighter, to hide the shaking of her hands.

'Cassy?'

Robert looked at her, with a frown. But before he could say anything else, Lyall came roaring down the road in the Moongazer van.

Thank goodness! Even if it *was* Lyall, she was glad to see him. Anything to get her out of this awkward situation. Cassy waved wildly and the van screeched along the kerb and stopped beside them.

'Hi!'

Lyall jumped out, locked the door and fell into step beside them. 'How did you get on?'

'Not bad.' Robert grinned. 'We've made millions of notes, about all sorts of terrible things. There's sure to be something in there that will fill in the gaps. I think we're all set for Monday now.'

Lyall pulled a face. 'Oh no we're not. I've just been to Wandsworth—and Earl's broken his leg.'

Robert's grin vanished. 'Badly?'

'Oh, he's OK.' Lyall shrugged. 'But he's not going to be moving about much for the next few weeks.'

'There must be someone else who can paint for us,' Robert said briskly. 'What about that girlfriend of Jacob's? Isabel Something.'

It was like living with a filing cabinet, Cassy thought. Or a computer. Whatever they needed to know, Robert had a file to cover it. Up it had popped, immediately he wanted it: 'Alternative Painters to Use when Earl Breaks His Leg'.

(Had he got one labelled 'What to Do about Plastic Explosive inside Masks'?)

But Lyall wasn't interested in Robert's efficiency. He flapped it away impatiently. 'Oh it's not that. A bit of plaster won't stop him waving a paintbrush around. It's the actual show that's in trouble. Who are we going to have for the third little pig?'

'But that's no problem.' Robert glanced at Cassy. 'I mean, we can—'

For a second, Cassy didn't realize what he meant. When she did, she almost shrieked. 'Me? I'm not going to take his place! It hasn't got anything to do with me!'

'Why not?' Robert said. 'You're living here, aren't you? Eating our food? Why not help to earn the money?'

'But I can't act!'

'It's not like acting. You only have to do what Lyall tells you.'

They weren't exactly shouting, but they were standing still on the pavement, facing each other. Robert looked exasperated, as if Cassy was being childish. And Cassy was absolutely enraged. It was bad enough to have to live with Goldie's peculiar friends, without having to join in their play-acting. Especially now . . .

Lyall put an arm round each of them. 'Knock it off, you two! Before I bang your heads together!'

'But you can't expect—'

Cassy tried to pull away from him, but he squeezed her harder and gave her shoulder a little shake.

'I can expect *anything*. Expecting things from schoolkids is what I do for a living. OK?'

'But I'm not a schoolkid, am I?' Cassy hissed. 'I'm not allowed to go to school! I have to be here, in this—this *slum*, with you and Goldie. Not having proper meals. Not sleeping in a proper bed. Not behaving like a real person at all.'

She hadn't realized that she was beginning to shout. Not until she stopped, and there was sudden silence. Lyall and Robert were both staring at her.

'What *is* this thing you've got about real life?' Robert said quietly. '*Real* life and *real* people? That doesn't mean anything. It's just a way of making walls, to shut out what's uncomfortable. And it doesn't work, you know. If things are there, you have to admit it in the end.'

Cassy caught her breath. That was too close. As though he had seen into her mind. She turned her head away quickly, to stop him watching her eyes.

'I think we've all had enough for today.' Lyall's arm tightened round her shoulders. 'Suppose we go in and have supper and then settle for an early night?'

Cassy nodded, but Robert's words were still trumpeting in her head. *If things are there, you have to admit it in the end.*

*   *   *

. . . there was the cottage at last, across the clearing. No dark figure was waiting at the gate. No footsteps sounded from the other path. Nothing moved except the woodsmoke rising from the chimney.

And yet—

Did the door always stand ajar? Was there always a line of shadow down the edge? What was inside, hidden in the darkness?

What was inside?

She began to run across the clearing, towards the cottage. Her feet slid on the damp grass. The heavy basket dragged at her arm. Her left hand was lifted, ready to knock on the door. Faster and faster and faster she ran.

Without getting any closer . . .

CHAPTER 11

'Cassy!'

It was Goldie. She was kneeling on the floor, tugging at the blankets.

'What's up?' Cassy muttered, sitting up sleepily.

'Nothing's *up*,' Goldie said. 'We're just ready to start.'

'Start what?'

'Rehearsal, of course. How are we going to get you ready for Monday unless we practise and practise and practise?'

She jumped to her feet and began to dance round the room with small, neat steps, clicking her fingers. Her hair swished and her bare feet thudded softly on the floorboards.

Cassy frowned. 'I never said I was doing it.'

'Don't be silly. Who's going to do it if you don't?'

'That's not my problem—'

'And we have to have the money.' Goldie gave a hop, a skip and a jump, that took her across the front of the window and round towards the fireplace. 'No Moongazing, no food.'

She stopped with her back to the room, staring at the mantelpiece. Slowly, Cassy pulled on her clothes, translating what Goldie had said into Nan's language. *You've got to pay your way in this world. You can't just sponge off other people.*

'But you don't understand,' she said crossly, to Goldie's back. 'I'm no good at things like that.'

'Like what?' Goldie's mind had flitted on. She spun round, smiling and holding out the photograph from the mantelpiece. 'Can I have this, Cassy? Please? I haven't got any photos of Mick. And this one's so sweet.' She beamed at the photograph and gave it a little pat. 'You looked like that when you were a baby, you know. I did hope you'd grow up like him—and I always wanted us to be a real family.'

Cassy's whole body tightened. 'Why did you want me to be like him? He's not sweet now, is he?'

83

Goldie's smile vanished. She shrank back warily, as if Nan were telling her off and she didn't quite understand what she'd done.

Cassy clenched her fists. 'Tell me! Why won't anyone tell me? He's my father, and I need to know about him.'

'Granny Phelan said I mustn't.' Goldie's voice came out in a whisper. 'She said I'd never see you again if I did.'

'Tell me,' Cassy said relentlessly. 'Michael Phelan, the Cray Hill bomber—that's what Lyall called him. Did he kill people?'

Goldie hesitated.

'Oh come on! It would have been in the papers. On television.'

'But he said not to believe those.' Goldie spoke so softly that Cassy could hardly hear. '*Remember it's war* he said. *And the enemy runs the papers and the television.*'

'But what did they say?'

'I'm sure it was all lies—'

'*What* was?'

'All those people. All the women and babies and—'

Cassy closed her eyes, struggling not to make pictures, wishing she had never asked. She knew just what Nan would have said. *Happy now, Miss Need-to-know-it-all?*

But she did need to know. 'Was it the IRA?'

Goldie giggled nervously. 'Granny Phelan was furious. She didn't speak for three days when she found out. She kept us in her flat—you and me—but she never said a word.'

Cassy opened her eyes and saw the smile that went with the giggle. It was completely blithe and innocent. Goldie's mind had flitted over the dead babies, as if they were part of a story.

And the next moment it flitted again. She skipped over to the door, still clutching the photograph. 'Come up as soon as you're ready. Lyall wants to start now, and he hates hanging around. I'll get Rob to make you a bacon sandwich.'

There was no time to refuse, and it seemed pointless to argue anyway. Goldie smiled and slid out, shutting the door behind her.

Cassy stood facing the mantelpiece, shivering as she stared at the empty spot where the photograph had been. And not just the photograph. The lump of yellow stuff had been there too, lying innocently next to it, for anyone to see.

Her mind churned. Bombs and bodies and secret, midnight raids. Was any of it possible?

You don't want to believe Goldie's fairy stories.

But the magic words didn't work today. It was Nan who seemed like a fairy story. And the most certain—the *realest*—thing in the whole world was that lump of yellow explosive, hidden in the wolf's head.

Ten minutes later she was sitting cross-legged on the floor in the front bedroom. She and Robert and Goldie were facing Lyall, and all four of them were chanting in loud, steady voices, banging out the rhythm on the floor with the flat of their hands.

> '*WHO's afraid of the Big Bad Wolf,*
> *The Big Bad Wolf, the Big Bad Wolf?*
> *WHO's afraid of the Big Bad Wolf . . . ?*'

Cassy felt ridiculous. Her voice sounded thin and awkward and her hands tapped lightly, hardly making a sound. But that didn't satisfy Lyall. He held up a hand and stopped them all.

'Come on, Cassy. Screech it at the top of your voice. You're taunting the wolf. Letting him know he doesn't scare you. Think of the worst thing that you can possibly imagine, just outside the door. You'd yell then, wouldn't you?'

Oh no she wouldn't. She would keep very, very still and silent. But she didn't want to explain that to Lyall, so she started again.

'Who's afraid of the Big Bad—'

'No! Louder, Cassy. LOUDER. Break my eardrums.'

'*Who's afraid—*'

'LOUDER!!'

He battered at her until she couldn't stand it any longer. Until, out of sheer rage and irritation, she yelled the words back at him.

'WHO'S AFRAID OF THE BIG BAD WOLF?'

And then he was smiling. 'Great! Good girl!'

He waved to the others to join in with her and when they

did, Cassy was caught up in the noise. Her voice rose with theirs. Her hands battered the floor with the same relentless thuds. On and on and on, until the words had stopped making sense. Until their throats were dry and the palms of their hands were red and sore.

Then Lyall sprang to his feet, towering over the rest of them. 'Right! Let's get going on the play. Are you ready, little pigs?'

Goldie gave a long, delicious squeal. 'You did tell Earl that I want to be a *pretty* pig, didn't you?'

Lyall grabbed her hands and pulled her up. 'I certainly did. You're going to be the neatest, sweetest little Berkshire that anyone's ever seen.'

'And I'll build the best straw house in the world!'

'You bet.' Lyall spoke over her shoulder, explaining it to Cassy. 'We'll have the audience set up in three sections, sitting on the floor. And you'll actually be using the children to build your houses. A line of kids for each wall. OK?'

Cassy blinked. 'But how will they know what to do?'

'They'll be led. When it's not your turn to be a pig, you'll take off your mask and be part of the other pigs' houses.'

'But—'

'It's all right,' Robert said. 'It sounds impossible, but it'll work. You wait and see.'

Cassy couldn't believe it. If Lyall got the audience to stand up—how would he ever get them sitting down again? She imagined hundreds of children crashing around, out of control, running wild.

But no one else seemed to be bothered. Goldie had pulled on a pair of high-heeled shoes and she was pattering around with tiny little steps, as though she had hooves. Robert had begun a new page in his file, making notes about where everyone had to stand. And Lyall was wrapping a huge cloak round himself.

And then, without any particular fuss or bother, they had begun. Goldie skipped into the middle of the room, beamed round and said, 'I'm going to build a house of straw.'

Robert grabbed Cassy's hand, pulling her into place, and Goldie dabbed at them, pretending to build. Then she crouched down behind the wall they made, as Lyall advanced on them.

'Little pig, little pig,' he boomed at the top of his voice, 'let me come in!'

'No!' squealed Goldie. 'No, no! By the hair of my chinny-chin-chin! You can't come in!'

Cassy glanced over her shoulder and saw her cower and shudder, as Lyall's voice rose in a huge, deepening crescendo.

'Then I'll huff, and I'll *puff*, and I'LL BLOW YOUR HOUSE DOWN!'

He began to blow, miming the puffs with such force that Cassy hardly realized that he was muttering stage directions at the same time, under his breath.

'Huff! (Just shudder a bit, Cassy.) Puff! (Shudder harder now.) HUFF! (Now pull away from Robert, but don't let go—that's right. Good.) PUFF! (Now slip your hands apart—and away.)'

Robert's hand slid out of Cassy's and he whirled away to the right, tugging an imaginary line of children after him. Cassy copied, moving left rather more woodenly. And Goldie squealed.

'No! No! NO!'

Lyall leaped forward and, with another, ear-splitting scream, she disappeared under his cloak. Her terror was perfect, as though the whole thing were real and vivid in her head. Blood and pain and death.

But when it came to *real* blood and death . . .

'We've got to get that changeover as smooth as silk,' Lyall was saying. 'Goldie, make sure you whip off your pig mask the *minute* you're under the cloak. You pull yours on, Robert. And Cassy must get the kids to sit down again.'

'Me? But—'

Before she could argue, Goldie was pulling at her hand. 'We're going to be the house of sticks now,' she hissed. 'And Robert's going to be the pig. He's so funny!'

Cassy hadn't expected Robert to be a good actor, and in a way she was right. He simply walked into the middle of the room, pulled Cassy and Goldie into place, and pretended to nail them together.

He was as solemn and brisk as he always was, whether he was cooking the breakfast or copying out facts in the library. And Goldie was right. It was irresistibly funny.

At last he stood up, with his hands on his hips. 'I have built a fine house of sticks,' he announced.

This time there were no instructions from Lyall. He simply advanced on them and began his wolfish threats. And Cassy had to grip Goldie's hand very tightly, to stop herself flinching away. He was huge and fierce and he came much closer this time, yelling right into their faces. It was a relief to let go at last and whirl away.

There was no scream from Robert. He simply flung up his hands and disappeared under the cloak. Lyall gave a thunderous roar, more like a lion than a wolf.

'Now it's you,' Goldie muttered in Cassy's ear. 'You've got to build the brick house.'

Cassy froze. 'But I can't—'

'You don't need to act.' Robert slid out from under the cloak and gave her a quick, reassuring smile. 'Just pretend the bricks are there and you really are building a house. That's what I always do.'

'But I'm not building a real house,' Cassy said stubbornly.

Lyall grabbed her by the shoulders. 'For heaven's sake, girl! Imagine! You might be surprised by what you come up with. Let your mind go.'

Never, never. Cassy's mind closed tight, like a fist clenching, and she glared at Lyall.

'But it's easy, Cassy.' Goldie gave her an innocent, angelic smile. 'Just be like Granny Phelan. As if you're sure your house is the best.'

Cassy glared again, but she could feel her shoulders straightening and her chin lifting. As she began to pull Goldie and Robert into place, she felt exactly like Nan. She made the walls of her imaginary house straight and exact, and the corners perfectly square. Then she brushed off her hands and nodded, the way Nan did when she'd finished tidying up.

'*I've* built a house of bricks!'

Lyall smiled at her. 'That is *it*, Cassy. Now get yourself inside.'

She dived between Goldie and Robert, pulled them close together again, to shut the door, and crouched down. For a moment there was silence and then she heard Lyall's feet padding up and down in front of the house. Automatically, she crouched lower, hiding away behind her brick walls.

The footsteps stopped and the voice came at her, very deep and dark.

'Little pig, little pig, let me come in!'

CHAPTER 12

The wolf's jaws snapped, outside the wall. Snapped and went on snapping all through the long, exhausting morning. Whatever they did, it came back to the same murderous bite.

Death. Terror.

The Big Bad Wolf swallowed up the pigs, again and again, as they rehearsed the play.

Then Lyall settled to tell a story—and the nightmare teeth of the Fenriswolf snapped shut on the wrist of the god Tyr, biting off his hand.

And after that, they were into the real world and the stories were even bloodier and more horrific. Cassy and Goldie and Robert raced in, interrupting Lyall's talk about wolves to report like eyewitnesses.

'Russian wolves are attacking Napoleon's army as it retreats from Moscow!'

'Scottish wolves are digging up cemeteries to eat the corpses!'

'Indian wolves are carrying off babies!'

On and on and on. A litany of accusation from history and myth and folk-tales. Wolf, wolf, wolf. Fangs and claws. Terrible swift, tireless feet. Nightmare voices, baying at the moon.

And over and over again they chanted, leading an imaginary audience.

'Who's afraid of the Big Bad Wolf,
The Big Bad Wolf, the Big Bad Wolf . . . ?'

It should have been better after lunch. Once they had eaten their sandwiches, they moved on to rehearse the second section of the show.

'The lecture,' Lyall said. 'On behalf of the wolf himself.'

It sounded blessedly, blissfully dull. A matter of wallcharts and graphs and a single, droning voice. But Cassy saw, straightaway, that it wasn't going to be like that. The moment Lyall said *lecture*, Goldie gave a little skip of delight.

'Are we going to have the video? The one with the baby wolves?'

Lyall nodded. 'The video first. And then the facts.'

He drained his cup of coffee and stood up. Marching across the room, he pulled an armful of paper out of a box. Four or five long, white rolls, like posters. 'I'll do the chat, and I want you three reading these under your breath. All the time. When you get to the end, go back to the beginning and start again. But just mutter, unless I tap your shoulder.'

'Like I do in the Jungle show?' Goldie said.

'That's right. It has to be there in the background while I'm talking. And when I touch you I want it good and loud. Here.'

Deftly and dramatically, he unrolled his posters and stuck them on the wall. One of them was a map of the world, coloured to show the places where wolves were extinct. The others were just words.

Lists of parasites. Lists of sub-species hunted to death. Lists of traps and ways of killing.

'I'll do the parasites,' Cassy said quickly, before Lyall could give her something worse. At least the Latin names meant nothing to her. They would blot out the rest.

She stared at her poster, eyes fixed, ears closed. And the moment Lyall began to talk, she started to mutter, steadily and without any expression, as if she were a machine.

'The tapeworm *Diphyllobothrium latum*, the tapeworm *Dipylidium caninum*, the tapeworm *Echinococcus granulosus* . . .'

But it didn't work. She could still hear Robert, murmuring the names of animals that had been wiped out. And she could hear Goldie's clear, low voice swelling louder as Lyall touched her shoulder.

' . . . the ice-box trap, the edge trap, piercers, fishhooks . . .'

Pain, death, blood . . .

They worked steadily until six o'clock, checking every tiny detail of the show. Lyall made them practise over and over again, until he was certain that they had it perfect and Cassy knew what to do.

Cassy was exhausted. She stared at Robert as he took neat, careful notes, wondering how he had the strength to hold a pen.

'Have I got it all now?' he said. 'We start with putting them in groups and teaching them the chant. Then it's The Three Little Pigs and the story of Tyr. *Then* the myth-history, when we all run in and report.'

Lyall nodded. 'And after that you shell out the paper and get them to do the first set of pictures. We can mount those in the lunch hour.'

'No problem there.' Robert frowned and tapped his pen against his teeth. 'But what about the second lot of pictures? That's going to be a terrible rush—'

Goldie tugged at Lyall's sleeve. 'Have you got to do all that now? I'm starving, Lyall. Can't Robert get his boring old notes sorted out tomorrow?'

Lyall ruffled her hair and grinned at Robert. 'Got anything to eat?'

'There's some bread and cheese—'

'No more sandwiches!' wailed Goldie. 'I'm sick of sand-wiches. Can't we have something proper?'

Lyall pulled a face, ready to say no. Then he glanced at Cassy, and his expression changed. 'I think we're all pretty tired,' he said slowly. 'How about fish and chips? Shall I go down to Arnie's and get some?'

'Oh yes! And can I have a pickled egg?' Goldie was instantly bouncy again, smiling and pulling at his arm. 'And some mushy peas?'

Lyall glanced back at Cassy, but all he said was, 'You put the stuff away, Robert.'

Then he and Goldie were gone, laughing their way down the stairs. Cassy levered herself up off the floor and reached for one of the posters. Slowly and listlessly, she began to roll it up, struggling to keep the ends even.

'It's OK.' Robert took down the next poster. 'You can leave that. I'll do them.'

'No. No, I'm fine.'

'You don't look it. You look dead tired.'

'I said I'm fine!'

'OK, don't bite my head off.' Robert put down the roll he was holding and stared at her, not very sympathetically. 'You'll feel better if you stop sulking,' he said.

'But I'm not—'

'Don't give me that. I know you don't want to help out with the show. Kids don't have to earn their living in the *real* world, do they?'

'It's not that,' Cassy said. 'Honestly.'

'So what's eating you? You were pretty peculiar yesterday, come to think of it, and you've been prickly all day today.'

'I—oh, it's nothing.'

'So don't tell me.' Robert shrugged and turned his back on her, beginning to roll another poster. After a second or two, without turning round, he said. 'But you can tell me if you want to.'

'I—' Cassy stood and looked at his solid, sensible back. Then, very slowly, she said, 'I'm probably crazy.'

'Then I guess you do need to tell someone.'

'Well—you must promise to keep it a secret.'

Robert slid an elastic band on to the poster and then, at last, he did turn round. 'I'd be dumb to promise that. If you're going to tell, you've got to trust me to be sensible. Otherwise you're better keeping it to yourself.'

But she had gone too far to draw back. If only she had Nan— But Nan wasn't there.

'It's that yellow stuff,' she said abruptly. 'The stuff we put into the wolf's-head mask. I think it's some kind of plastic explosive.'

She half expected him to laugh at her, but he didn't. He sat down on the floor, with his knees drawn up to his chin. For a whole minute he rested his head there, thoughtfully. Then he looked up at her.

'Why?'

'Because—' Cassy closed her eyes and said it very fast, to get the worst bit over. 'Because my dad's a bomber. The police are after him. And Special Branch. And I think he's hiding out at Nan's.'

'What sort of bomber?'

'IRA. I think.'

93

'I see,' Robert said carefully. He thought for another moment and then began to fire crisp, quick questions at her. 'What makes you so sure he's there, in the flat?'

'I remembered where I heard that knock, the one that Goldie said was his special signal. Someone came to the flat and knocked like that. The night before Nan sent me here.'

'And why should you have the plastic explosive—if that's what it is?'

'I don't know,' said Cassy slowly. 'But I think he's trying to get it back. That man in the hood was him. The one who broke in. Goldie recognized him.'

'Goldie's always recognizing him. In shops, up ladders— everywhere. Didn't Lyall tell you?'

'Yes, but—' The more he argued, the more certain Cassy was. 'It all fits together, doesn't it? That peculiar yellow stuff. The knock. Nan sending me away. And the man trying to break in. It's got to mean something.'

'And you think your Nan's in on it?' Robert grinned and shook his head. 'So what is she? A colonel in the IRA? Come on, Cassy.'

'She's his mother,' muttered Cassy. 'And when I phoned her up—about the yellow stuff—she wouldn't talk to me. Mrs Ramage went to get her and she said she was too busy to come.'

'But you said you spoke to her.'

'I know I did,' Cassy mumbled. 'But it was a lie.'

Robert hugged his knees, not saying anything and after a moment she sat down beside him.

'What are you thinking? Am I mad?'

'I'm thinking—' He hesitated and then gave a small, wry smile. 'I'm thinking, *Things like that don't really happen. Not in the real world.*'

Cassy pulled a face. 'You weren't supposed to say that. You were supposed to say *Don't be daft, Cassy. Plastic explosive's not like that at all. It's bright purple with green spots and it smells of cooked cabbage and squeaks when you squeeze it.*'

Robert grinned sadly and shook his head. 'Sorry. It's yellow.'

They stared at each other, without speaking, until Cassy looked away.

'So what should I do?' she said. 'Ignore it all? Call the police? Take the stuff out of the mask and leave it on the pavement for him? *You're* not much use, are you?'

Robert pulled a face. 'It *can't* be true, can it? We can't really be sitting here talking about it like this. There's got to be a simple, straightforward explanation. Only—'

'Only what?' said Cassy. Not smiling.

'Only sometimes the horror stories are true.'

'And then?'

He frowned. 'And then, I guess, you have to work out which side you're on.' He looked up at Cassy. In quite a different voice, he said, 'Look, let's wait until after Monday. The stuff will be perfectly safe inside the mask. Plastic explosive doesn't go off without a detonator.'

'But we can't just—'

'We *need* the wolf's head,' Robert said firmly. 'And we haven't got time to make another one. Anyway, I guess we could both do with a day or two to get used to the idea.'

'And then?'

'And then we'll tell Lyall.'

'*Lyall?*'

'He'll know how to handle it.'

'But—'

There were a thousand questions rattling round in Cassy's head, but before she could ask any of them, the front door banged and Goldie's voice called up the stairs.

'Weren't we quick?'

'OK, then?' Robert hissed at Cassy. 'Is that the plan?'

'I suppose so.' Cassy swallowed. Tuesday was the day, then. On Tuesday, they would have to do something.

Feet thudded on the stairs and Goldie burst into the room. Her arms were full of warm white parcels of fish and chips and she was beaming all over her face.

'Food!'

Behind her came Lyall, a knife and fork in one hand and a plate in the other. With a fantastic, elaborate flourish, he bowed until his forehead almost touched the ground, holding them out to Cassy.

'For you! Gracious living!'

Cassy managed a small, stiff smile. She could see that he

meant to be kind, but he just seemed more impossible than ever. What would he do when they told him about the yellow stuff?

Lyall, there's a bomb in the wolf's head.

Still, perhaps Robert was right and she needed time. Perhaps it would be easier to think about when she had slept on it.

* * *

. . . her hand lifted to tap on the door, and as she knocked, it swung backwards, away from her.

Into the darkness.

And then again. The action repeated itself precisely. Her hand lifted and knocked. Two quick taps. Then a pause. Then two more. The door swung open wider.

And again. Her hand lifted. Knocked. The darkness gaped.

And again.

She did not know which of the knocks brought the answer. Once the words were spoken, it seemed they had always been there.

Come in . . .

CHAPTER 13

The knocking carried over from her dream and woke her, so that she caught her breath and sat up in the dark.

'Who's there?'

'It's us,' Robert said from the other side of the door. 'Time to get up. We're going in ten minutes.'

'Going?'

But he was already padding away down the hall, towards the kitchen. Cassy grabbed her clothes and began to pull them on. What was happening? Had somebody found the explosive?

Before she had finished, there was more knocking, harder this time. And the voice that called to her was Lyall's.

'Aren't you ready yet? Come on! We ought to be leaving.'

'Why?'

But he wasn't going to tell her. He pulled the door open, so that Cassy could just make out his solid, dark shape in the hall. 'Hurry! You'll find out soon enough.'

Cassy did up the last button of her blouse. 'Can't I wash my face?'

'Oh for heaven's sake! We're not going to see the Queen.' She could hear how he was fuming. 'You can have thirty seconds and that's it. But I'll flay you alive if we're too late.'

'Too late for what?'

'You'll see.'

He marched off to open the front door. Cassy ran down the hall, into the kitchen. There was a candle standing on one of the boxes and, by its dim light, Robert was pushing a heap of sandwiches into a bag.

'Breakfast in the van,' he said briskly.

'But what—?'

'No time to explain now.'

Then he was gone too, leaving Cassy to splash her face hastily with water from the tap. She had forgotten her towel, but she didn't dare to go back and fetch it, because she could hear Lyall starting up the engine. Grabbing her mac, she ran out into the dark street.

The van door was open, waiting for her, as she raced down the front path. She jumped into the passenger seat and they were away before she had slammed the door. Glancing over her shoulder, she saw Robert, crouched in the back of the van.

'Where's Goldie?'

'You must be joking!' Lyall gave a great bellow of laughter. 'We'll be *back* before Goldie wakes up.'

'Back from what?'

'Never you mind.' He looked back at Robert, steering wildly round a corner at the same time. 'Here, give her a sandwich. She needs something to occupy her mind.'

Robert pushed a fat, cheese sandwich over Cassy's shoulder and she sat glowering as she chewed it, wondering why she had come. They had just bounced her into it, making her run around before she was properly awake. Even Robert wouldn't tell her what was going on.

The van careered down the middle of roads and round corners in an eerie scramble through the back streets. There was hardly another vehicle in sight and, looking round, Cassy realized that it was very early indeed. Four o'clock? Even three o'clock, maybe.

But they weren't early enough for Lyall. He drove at top speed all the way until, with one final lurch, they came up against a barrier and he switched off the engine.

'We're here.'

Cassy stared, suddenly recognizing the place. 'The *zoo*?' Nothing to do with bombs, then. She was so relieved that she almost laughed. 'But what are we doing here? It's shut.'

Lyall grinned. 'Let's break in, shall we?'

For one frenzied moment, Cassy almost believed him. Suppose they had come to kidnap a wolf. Anything seemed possible now. The scene that played itself over in her head was as sharp as a nightmare, and horribly plausible.

She could see Lyall outside the wolf enclosure, with a stun gun in his hand. He fired and a wolf slumped to the ground as the dart hit it. Then—skeleton keys to open the cage. And

Lyall would bundle the wolf into a sack while she and Robert held off the other five wolves.

Then Robert reached over the back of her seat and put a hand on her shoulder. 'It's all right. It's all been properly organized.'

'I can sweet-talk myself into *anywhere* if I need to.' Lyall laughed. 'Just let me check in.'

He slid out of the van and, for the first time, Cassy noticed the shadowy figure of a man beside the barrier. He raised a hand and came forward.

As Lyall went to meet him, Cassy turned round and hissed at Robert. 'Why can't you tell me what's going on?'

He shook his head. 'You'll be pleased we didn't tell you beforehand. Just wait and see.'

'How do you know what I'm going to be pleased about?'

But Lyall was back, and the next moment they were driving under the lifted barrier, into the zoo.

'Mr Marriott says we must get our stuff in place fast,' muttered Lyall. 'To avoid disturbing them later on.'

What stuff? In the darkness it was hard to see what Lyall and Robert pulled out of the back of the van, but Cassy found herself holding three microphones and a bundle of leads.

'We'll get set up,' Lyall murmured, 'and then we'll find somewhere to wait, out of sight.'

'Out of sight of *what*?' But Cassy did not expect anyone to tell her. Lyall and Robert just grinned at each other, annoyingly, and walked into the zoo, each carrying a large box. All Cassy could do was follow them, and see what happened.

An hour later, she was no wiser. She was sitting on the cold, hard tarmac, round the corner from the wolf enclosure, with Robert on one side and Lyall on the other. They had fussed over microphones, tested sound levels and argued over the best place to wait.

But nothing had happened. The only difference was that the darkness had given way to a chilly grey light.

Cassy was beginning to think the whole thing was some elaborate practical joke. Perhaps they would sit there for another hour, and then Lyall would ask her what she had *expected* to hear. And, whatever she answered, she would look like an idiot.

Or perhaps he was making a recording to show that wolves didn't snore. That was just the sort of crazy idea that would take his fancy.

Wriggling awkwardly on the hard ground, she decided to ignore the whole thing. Instead of wondering why they were there, she began to run over the Wolf Show in her mind. If she had to be in it, she was going to do her bits as well as she could. So she made a mental list of all her moves and tried to remember all the words she had to say. Rumours about wolves . . . parasites of wolves . . . pictures of wolves . . .

The real wolves took her by surprise.

Suddenly, from round the corner, came a whine followed by a long, low moan that prickled the hairs on her neck. She began to scramble up, but Lyall was ready for that. One of his huge hands grabbed the back of her neck, forcing her down again, and he put a finger fiercely to his lips.

The moan broke off and started again, not alone this time. Other voices joined in, but they did not keep together. The pitches shifted constantly, each one avoiding all the others. Chords and discords formed and dissolved and formed anew in strange, mournful patterns.

Cassy swallowed and sat up straight. The sound wasn't singing, but it caught at her ears like rough music, with a ragged, irregular harmony.

As the moans grew higher and shorter, Lyall let go of her hand and began to crawl towards the corner. Robert followed, grinning at Cassy and beckoning her until she crept into the space beside Lyall.

Now they could see round the corner, into the wolf enclosure. The six wolves were standing in a circle on top of the mound, facing outwards. Their muzzles were lifted to the sky and their eyes were narrowed, ecstatically, as they howled. Cassy dug her fingernails into the palms of her hands, willing them not to stop. She wanted the beautiful, inhuman noise to go on for ever.

But, one by one, the voices died away until the last one drew out its final, solitary howl. Then that last wolf, too, dropped its head and trotted slowly from the mound. Cassy realized that she was trembling.

Lyall took two quick steps to the tape recorder and switched it off. Then he turned and grinned triumphantly. 'There! Did you guess what we were waiting for, Cassy?'

She shook her head, because she couldn't speak yet.

'And wasn't it better like that? When you don't know what you're hearing—you really *hear* it.'

'I thought—' Her voice cracked but she forced it back to steadiness. 'I thought they only did that at night. At the full moon.'

Robert nodded. 'That's why we didn't tell you. We didn't want you to expect something out of a horror film.'

'Ho-o-o-o-owling!' Lyall flung his head back with a blood-curdling moan. 'Snow driving over the steppes of Siberia! Ravening jaws, with fangs dripping gore!! Feet padding under the trees, following through the shadows and then—LEAPING!'

His eyes gleamed and, just for a second, a shape leaped in Cassy's mind. An elongated, obscene figure, with coarse grey hair and a fierce, fanged muzzle.

'Don't be soft,' she said shakily, waving her hand at the wolf enclosure. 'These wolves aren't like that.'

'Oh, ten out of ten!' Lyall clapped softly. 'No, these are howling to show they're here. To warn other wolves to keep off their territory.'

'Pathetic, really,' Robert muttered. 'You'd think they would realize it's a lost cause.'

Lyall shrugged. 'Lots of people fight for lost causes. Especially when it's to do with territory.'

Cassy bent down, suddenly, and pulled the microphone lead out of the tape recorder. 'Don't you think we ought to clear up? Or do you want to spend all day at the zoo?'

'Why not?' Lyall said, in a light, dangerous voice. 'Or don't you like it, Cassy?'

Her skin prickled, but before he could ask the question again, Robert bent down and began to coil the lead. 'Oh come on, Dad. Let's go back. We're all tired, and I'm ready for another breakfast.'

'You could *wolf* it down, could you?' The awkwardness evaporated as Lyall laughed. He loped round the corner, to collect the microphones, and Cassy and Robert packed up the tape recorder.

The journey home was slower, because of the traffic. They passed the time planning how to wake up Goldie.

'We could all howl outside the door,' Robert suggested. 'Like a pack of wolves.'

'Not a hope,' said Lyall. 'We'll have to go round the back and chuck stones at the window. That might do it, as long as we break the window.'

'We could—' Cassy visualized the back of the house. 'We could bang on that long drainpipe that goes past the window.'

'Great!' Lyall took his hands off the wheel, terrifyingly, and clapped. 'The drainpipe's bound to come away in our hands. So we can stick it through the hole in the window and yell in her ear.'

'We could tickle her with it, too,' Robert said solemnly. 'If it's long enough to reach across the room.'

'Or blow it—' Cassy spluttered, '—like a didgeridoo.'

But they didn't need to do anything. When they reached Albert Street, Goldie was awake already. Not only awake, but dressed and waiting on the front doorstep for them. The moment she saw the van, she began to wave, grinning furiously.

'What on earth—?' Lyall sounded puzzled. Pulling in to the kerb, he jumped out and called to her. 'What's the matter. What woke you up?'

'No one—I mean, nothing,' Goldie called back, brightly. 'I woke up all by myself. Honestly. And . . . '

Cassy got out and went to the back of the van, to undo the doors for Robert. As he swung his legs out, he pulled a face at her.

'What's up with Goldie?'

Listening, Cassy realized what he meant. Goldie was still talking, twice as fast as usual, with a false, brittle brightness that left no space for anyone else to speak.

' . . . I thought I'd surprise you and make something to eat when you came in, but I haven't quite had time . . . '

'Perhaps she was frightened,' Cassy muttered back. 'Because we left her like that.'

'Perhaps.' Robert looked doubtful. 'Here, give us a hand with these leads, will you?'

He and Cassy finished unloading the van and took the equipment to the front bedroom. As they walked back down, Robert gave Cassy a friendly grin.

'Lyall and Goldie are making coffee and toast. Want some? Or would you rather get a bit more sleep?'

'I'm not sleepy at all.' Cassy jumped down the last two steps. 'I'll just put my mac away.'

She crossed the hall, pushed her door open—and stopped dead. There was something wrong. A primitive sense, more basic than sight or smell, set the skin prickling all over her body.

Someone had been in her room while they were out.

CHAPTER 14

She must have stood still for longer than she realized, because Robert suddenly stopped half-way to the kitchen, and glanced round.

'Are you OK?'

'I—yes. Yes, of course.'

He hesitated, then walked back. 'No you're not. You look weird.'

'Somebody's been in my room,' Cassy said, in a low, stiff voice. 'Somebody's been going through my things.'

Robert glanced over her shoulder. 'Are you sure?'

He didn't believe her, and it was easy to see why. The room was perfectly tidy, the way she always left it, with her blankets folded on the floor and her case neatly closed. Nothing had been taken away, or moved to a different place. And yet—

'Everything's in parallel lines,' she said slowly. 'See? The blankets are folded perfectly square, and they've been laid down with the edges parallel to the floorboards. And the side of the case is parallel to that. *And* my sponge bag. *And* the packet of postcards on top of the case.'

Robert didn't look convinced. 'But why would anyone do that?'

'I don't know.' Cassy frowned at the rigorous pattern of lines. 'Perhaps—without realizing? Just trying to leave the room tidy?'

'You could have done it yourself then. You are incredibly tidy. Maybe you always line things up, without noticing.'

'Then why does it look so strange to me? And anyway—' Cassy realized it in a rush, '—even if I did fold my blankets this morning, I couldn't have lined them up like that. It was too dark to see.'

Robert frowned. 'Maybe it happened by accident.'

Cassy didn't bother to reply to that. She knew it hadn't, and so did he.

104

'Hang on.' Robert turned and called down the hall. 'Goldie, were you in all the time we were out?'

Goldie appeared in the kitchen doorway, very quickly. 'Yes. Of course I was. Why?'

'Don't ask—' Cassy muttered under her breath.

But Robert ignored her. 'Did anyone come? Cassy thinks someone's been in her room.'

'Oh. Yes.' Goldie turned suddenly pink and gave a quick, high-pitched laugh. 'Sorry, Cassy. It was me. I just—wanted a pair of scissors to cut my nails.'

Cassy looked down the hall. Even from where she was standing, she could see Goldie's long, polished nails. They were varnished red, and the varnish was chipped at the ends. 'Have you done it now?' she said carefully. 'Can I have my scissors back?'

'Oh!' Goldie laughed again, a little breathlessly. She glanced down at her hands, following Cassy's eyes. 'I didn't find them. So I couldn't cut my nails after all.'

Cassy looked at the red nails very hard for a moment. 'I'll get them,' she said quickly, turning away so that Goldie shouldn't see her face. 'Wait a moment.'

Robert followed her, without needing to be asked, and stood beside her as she knelt in front of her case. Without looking at him, she lifted the lid. The nail scissors were where she expected them to be, where she had left them the night before.

Right on top, in the middle.

'Even Goldie couldn't have missed those,' she said, very quietly. 'Could she?'

Robert didn't answer, but when Cassy glanced up at him he shook his head. His thin, dark face was stony and for a moment she thought she still had to convince him.

'Goldie never made my room as tidy as that, either,' she hissed. 'She wouldn't know a parallel line if it bit her.'

Robert shook his head again, but he still did not speak.

'So?' said Cassy. 'Who was it? What did he want?'

Robert swallowed. 'It must have been—him. Looking for the explosive. He must have seen us go out.'

'And—Goldie let him in?'

They stared at each other, and Robert nodded slowly. 'Must have done.'

Cassy felt both their minds change gear, at the same second. *It's really true. In real life.* There was no need to say it out loud.

She stood up. 'What shall we do? Are we still going to wait until Tuesday?'

Robert swallowed and shook his head. 'We ought to do something now. Let's try phoning your grandmother again. Before we rush into anything drastic.'

'All right.' Cassy closed her eyes, working out days and times. 'It's no use now, though. She'll be at the hospital. I mean—she's supposed to be.'

'What about this evening? We'll go out to buy some fish and chips, and then we won't need to explain ourselves to Lyall.'

'OK. I suppose so.' Cassy didn't really want to wait. She wanted to race off, straightaway, and find out what was going on. But she could see that it was sensible. 'What shall we do until then, to take our minds off it?'

'Don't be daft!' Robert grinned, suddenly and disconcertingly. 'We'll be rehearsing, of course.'

Cassy pulled a face when he said it, but she was very glad of the rehearsal. It kept them so busy that they couldn't worry, or talk about anything else. From nine o'clock in the morning until six o'clock at night, they were doing what Lyall said, speaking the words he gave them and moving where he pointed.

Cassy got so absorbed that she was actually surprised at six o'clock, when Robert said, 'Fish and chips, OK? Cassy and I will go to the shop.'

'Are you sure?' Lyall stood up. 'I've got to go over to Earl's anyway, so I could nip round in the van—'

'We need the walk,' Robert said, firmly. 'Come on, Cassy.'

He grabbed her hand, pulling her to her feet, and Lyall went down the stairs with them.

'Want a lift, then?'

Cassy gathered her wits. 'No thanks. I could do with a bit of fresh air. And anyway, we don't want to be too quick, or your fish will get really cold.'

Lyall grinned and leaped off down the hall. By the time Cassy and Robert reached the pavement, the van was already screeching away from the kerb, with Lyall's hand waving out of the window.

They walked side by side, down the road towards the phone box, but they didn't talk. Glancing sideways, Cassy could almost hear what Robert was thinking. *. . . not enough evidence to make up our minds yet . . . bound to be some simple explanation . . .* He was frowning, and he stared hard at the ground as he walked, chewing his bottom lip.

Cassy was beginning to wonder about it, too. The whole idea still seemed wild and unlikely. She couldn't really imagine talking to Nan about bombs and burglaries. Surely things like that would evaporate at the sound of her steady, sensible voice.

If only she could hear it! It seemed weeks—months—since Nan had said goodbye to her at the front door of the flat. Since then, the world had gone wrong, and Cassy was homesick for common sense.

The two of them went into the phone box together and Robert pulled some money out of his pocket.

'Here. Use this.'

'Thanks.' Cassy's hands shook as she pushed the coins into the slot and pressed the buttons. *Please let Nan be there. Please, please, please . . .*

The ringing went on and on, and she was almost ready to give up before Mrs Ramage's voice came, faintly, from the other end.

'Hallo?'

'It's me again, Mrs Ramage. Cassy. Can I speak to Nan?'

'Who is it? I'm afraid it's a very bad line.'

'It's *Cassy*. From next door.'

'Oh, Cassy. Hallo, dear. Are you having a nice little holiday?'

'Yes, thank you.' Cassy struggled not to sound impatient. 'Please could you fetch Nan for me?'

Mrs Ramage hesitated. 'I haven't seen her around for a while, dear. I think she must be away, too.'

Cassy's heart thudded once, very hard. 'I'm sure she's not. And I do need to speak to her. Please.'

'But I've just had a bath.' Mrs Ramage sounded hurt, as though Cassy ought to have guessed. 'I'm in my night things.'

'It's very, very important.' Cassy closed her eyes and took a deep breath. Nan would be furious with her for annoying Mrs Ramage, but it couldn't be helped. 'Can't you put on a coat and nip round? Please?'

There was a long and not very pleasant pause. Then Mrs Ramage sniffed. 'Well, I suppose I'll have to, if it's that important. But if you're going to keep phoning like this, she'd better get the phone put in herself.'

'Thank you,' Cassy said, as meekly as she could manage. 'I'll phone back in five minutes.'

She put the receiver down and leaned back against the side of the phone box. Robert watched her, but neither of them spoke. They were waiting to make the second call.

Mrs Ramage's words were rattling round in Cassy's head. *. . . I haven't seen her around for a while—she must be away . . .* But Nan never went anywhere, except to work, or to the shops—or to visit Goldie. Cassy couldn't remember her ever mentioning holidays or friends. She *had* to be there.

'That's five minutes,' Robert said, in a low voice. 'Are you going to ring again?'

She took a deep breath and fed some more money into the slot. This time, Mrs Ramage answered quickly and spoke before Cassy could say anything. She sounded breathless and irritated.

'It's just like I told you, dear. She's not there. I rang three times, but there was no answer. And there's no light in the hall.'

Cassy gripped the receiver and answered very carefully in an even, emotionless voice. 'Thank you for trying. I'm sorry I disturbed you.'

'I don't mind if it's really important,' Mrs Ramage said grudgingly. And then, more sharply and inquisitively, she added, 'Is there something wrong, dear?'

'No. It's all right. I mean—I'm fine. I'll write her a letter. Goodbye.'

Cassy rang off, rather too quickly for politeness, and took a long, deep breath.

'Not there?' Robert said.

'It's really peculiar.' Cassy suddenly found it difficult to breathe. 'Last time, Nan was in when she should have been out. And she wouldn't speak to me. This time she's out when she should be in.'

'Maybe she's swapped her duties. Or perhaps she's visiting a friend. Or gone down the pub.'

That was so funny that Cassy actually smiled, rather wearily. 'Let's go and get the fish and chips. There's nothing else we can do just now.'

'You don't want to talk it over?'

'Not yet.'

They walked round the corner and into the steamy warmth of the chip shop. Cassy's head was buzzing and the words of the menu danced in front of her eyes. Over them, weaving in and out, her questions sprawled all over the walls.

> *Cod and—where can Nan be?*
> *Huss—she's never out—chips.*
> *Is she OK? Surely HE wouldn't—and chips.*
> *Plaice and chips.*
> *Sausages and—what on earth are we going to do?*

The last question ran over and over in her head, behind everything else, without stopping. *What are we going to do? What CAN we do?* It wrote itself over the chip paper and beat with the rhythm of Cassy and Robert's feet as they walked home.

Neither of them spoke, until they were back in Albert Street. Then Robert nodded down the road, towards the house. 'Lyall's been quick. The van's back already.'

'Oh. Good.' Cassy muttered, not really listening.

But it was Goldie who opened the door, with her usual, innocent beam. 'Wonderful. I'm *starving*. Cassy, will you go up and get Lyall? He's in the mirror room.'

'Aren't we going to eat up there?' Robert took a step towards the stairs, but Goldie caught at his sleeve.

'That's not what Lyall said. He said *Get Cassy to come up and fetch me.*'

Robert looked baffled. 'But why?'

'It's what he *said*,' Goldie repeated obstinately. 'Go on, Cassy.'

Cassy's mind was still busy with other things. She had only vaguely heard what they were saying, but it seemed easier to go than to argue. She ran up the stairs and tapped on the door of the back bedroom. There was no answer, so she pushed it open to see if Lyall was still there.

He was standing by the window, with his back to her, looking out into the garden. His tracksuit hood was pulled up over his head and he was hunched slightly forward so that he could lean on the window-sill.

'Lyall—'

He turned.

For a split second, her brain froze, putting everything into slow motion. Repeating the same image, over and over again.

He turned—and instead of his face, there was a senseless, nightmare shape.

He turned—and the yellow teeth gnashed suddenly as his jaw snapped open.

He turned—and the long, grey muzzle flickered at her from every mirror in the room, at a hundred different angles, tinted blue, or pink, or yellow.

He turned—

Cassy screamed.

Wolf!

The wolf where no wolf should be. Behind the door, invading the house, inside the skin of a familiar, trusted person—

Werewolf. Bzou. *Loup garou*, ligahoo, lagahoo—nightmare babble for a nightmare from the dark corners of the mind.

Cassy's throat strangled with terror. Her body was rigid with it. Every ounce of energy, every fibre of her muscles, every breath from her lungs went into that one, long, uncontrollable scream.

It was only for a moment. Even before she had run out of breath, she could hear Goldie shrieking from downstairs.

'Cassy! Cassy, darling! What's happened?'

Goldie was running. Robert was running. And Lyall was pulling off the wolf mask. Sensible, ordinary life was there, all around her. There *was* no werewolf. Stupid, stupid, *stupid*—

She staggered dizzily, but Robert was there to catch her. 'That was bloody irresponsible!' she heard him say to Lyall. 'She's not used to playing your games. And she's got enough to cope with, without that.'

'No, no—' Cassy gulped air, trying to give a sensible

explanation. With no werewolves. 'It's only—that head's so dangerous—with that stuff we put inside—'

Robert's arm tightened round her shoulders, but for a moment she was too muzzy to make sense of the warning. She repeated what she had said, so that he wouldn't guess how stupid she had been.

'You know. That *yellow* stuff.'

For a second she could see them all, staring at her. Robert was frowning, Lyall had his head on one side and Goldie was in the doorway with her mouth wide open. None of it made any sense. Then Lyall bent down and switched off the tape recorder in the corner. 'So what's up with you guys?' he said softly.

It was Goldie who answered. She came suddenly to life and swept across the room, pushing Robert away from Cassy. 'What do you *think* is up?' she said furiously. 'You've terrified her, Lyall. *Look* at her!' Putting an arm round Cassy's waist, she led her across to the mattress. 'Come on, Cassy. Sit down and have a rest.'

Not very scientific treatment for shock, Cassy thought, wryly. Nan would have been off like a flash, to make a hot, sweet drink. But Goldie's arm was surprisingly comforting, and she leaned against it for a moment before she sat down.

Lyall grinned ruefully at Cassy. Ruefully—and rather curiously. 'I reckon we're all over-tired. Nip down and bring the food up here, Rob. And we'll have an early night when we've eaten.'

'And I'll take *this* thing out of the way,' Goldie said. With a sudden, sharp movement, she bent down and scooped up the wolf mask. 'I'll put it in the front bedroom.'

Cassy leaned her head against the wall and watched Goldie and the mask disappearing through the door.

* * *

. . . the room looked the same—but not the same. The fire flickered, sending jagged black shapes darting round the walls. Staining everything dull red and throwing

111

grotesque shadows across the face on the pillow.
Impossible shadows . . .

. . . the eyes under the frilled nightcap gleamed large
and luminous, flickering with the movement of the
flames . . .

. . . the huge eyes gleamed, drawing her nearer and
nearer, step by step, towards the high, soft bed . . .

Grandmother, what big eyes you have . . .

CHAPTER 15

Cassy knew, as soon as she opened her eyes, that it was very early. The light that filtered past the blanket in the window was thin and pale, and the air was clammy.

But it was no use trying to sleep again. The huge, staring eyes of her dream had woken her up too well. Pulling the mac round her shoulders, she went across to the window and lifted a corner of the blanket. Outside, the street was grey and empty, but there was a hint of brightness in the sky. It would be a good day for their journey to Berkshire.

Automatically, she glanced down the road, towards the Moongazer van. It was parked a few doors away, with its back to her. Idly, she followed the pattern of branches that twined round the rear windows, trying to spot the little differences between the painted trees.

It was a moment or two before she saw the man. He must have been standing in the road, beside the driver's door, bending forward over the bonnet. But when he straightened, she caught sight of the top of his head, muffled in a hood.

Before the image was clear in her mind, he came round on to the pavement and began jogging away from her, with an unmistakable, lop-sided gait. One shoulder higher than the other. Very light on his feet.

Cassy's mouth went dry. For the first time in her life, she recognized her father. So still that she was barely breathing, she stood and watched him lope down the road and away round the corner.

It was only when he vanished that she wondered why he had come. Buttoning her mac, she pushed her feet into her trainers. Then she tiptoed out of the room and began to wrestle with the bolts on the front door, sliding them open as quietly as she could.

She did not see the folded piece of paper until she actually

113

reached the van. It was tucked under one of the windscreen wipers and addressed to her, in small, square capitals.

CAITLIN PHELAN

Carefully, she lifted the wiper and took the piece of paper. The short and cryptic message was horribly clear to her.

> *Dear Red Riding Hood,*
> *I don't know what you did with the things in that basket of food, but one of them was very important. Without it, your grandmother will certainly die. Within twenty-four hours.*
> *Bring it back at once. AND BE SURE NOT TO TALK TO ANYONE ON THE WAY.*
> *Love from*
> *The Big Bad Wolf*

Cassy stood and read it two or three times, rolling one corner of the paper in her fingers. It was crazy. It was like some dreadful horror film, with knives and guns and bombs round every corner. It was—

It was real.

And she had to make herself believe that. Or, within twenty-four hours, Nan could be dead.

Slowly, she walked back down the road, folding the piece of paper as she went and feeling the big words in her mind. Death. Murder. Bombs.

Nan.

As she turned down the front path, she saw that Robert was standing in the doorway waiting for her. He didn't call out, but waited until she was right in front of him. Then he spoke, in a very low voice.

'I heard you go out. What's up? Couldn't you sleep?'

Cassy didn't answer. She simply handed the piece of paper to him. He glanced down at it, frowning as he saw the name written on the outside.

'Who—?'

'Me. Written the Gaelic way.'

His mouth twisted into a small, wry smile. 'That's as good as a signature, isn't it?' Then he unfolded the paper and began to read.

Cassy watched him carefully, but his expression didn't give her any clues. His eyes flicked from side to side as he read the note and then up to the top as he read it for a second time.

At last, he folded it up, creasing it sharply along the original folds with his fingernails.

'Well?' Cassy said.

She wanted him to gasp with horror. To do something to match the way she felt. But she should have known better. He began working everything out, in his usual, careful way.

'Why this cloak-and-dagger stuff then?'

'What do you mean?'

'Well, if he really wants it back, why not get your grandmother to write and ask for it?'

'Because she wouldn't do it,' Cassy said firmly. 'Why do you think she slipped it in that bag in the first place? If she doesn't want him to have it she won't do a thing to help him.'

'Hmm.' Robert nodded and weighed that up. 'So how did he know where to find you?'

'He—' For a moment, Cassy floundered, and then it came to her. '*I* told him! I sent a postcard—'

Nan had given her postcards so that she wouldn't put her address. But Goldie had moved. So when the postcard fell through the door on to Nan's mat . . .

Cassy closed her eyes, trying not to imagine the unknown hand that had been stretched out to pick it up. 'What are we going to do?'

'It'll have to be the police,' Robert said gently. 'This isn't the sort of thing you can mess about with.'

They were almost the words Nan had used, after the last IRA bomb report on the News. *Turn it off, Cassy*, she had said. *There's enough trouble in the world without that*. And when Cassy argued that she ought to know about it, Nan's voice had sharpened. *That's not something for you to mess around with!* Then she had marched off, into the kitchen, and sat on her own for a long time, with her head on the table.

Just another forbidden subject, like all the others. But now Cassy had to think about it. And she knew what she ought to do—what Nan would tell her to do.

'Yes,' she said, forcing herself to speak the words. 'We've got to call the police. Let's do it now. Where shall we start?'

Better to get it over with. Better not to start thinking about Nan in danger. About the deadly yellow lump that could save her—and kill someone else.

Robert pulled her inside and shut the door. 'We'll start by telling Lyall. He'll know what to do.'

'Lyall?'

Robert stiffened, very slightly, and stepped back. 'I know you don't like him, but he's no fool. You haven't seen him in a crisis. He'll know what to do. And he is grown up. The police are more likely to listen to him.'

'I suppose so.'

Reluctantly, Cassy followed Robert into the house and up the stairs. As they reached the door of the mirror room, he waved her on, along the landing.

'I'll wake Lyall up and explain, but he'll never believe us unless he sees the stuff. Can you go and cut it out of the mask?'

'OK.' As he raised his hand to knock, Cassy walked along the landing and into the front bedroom.

All four masks were lying on the floor. The three little pigs were side by side, carefully lined up against the wall. The wolf mask was further away, on its own.

Cassy stood and stared down at it for a second, catching an echo of the terror she had felt the day before. Now that it was painted, the exaggerated shape had taken on a nightmare reality. Earl had made the teeth a dirty yellow and tipped some of them with red. The bulging eyes stared and the nostrils at the end of the long muzzle were a gaping, cavernous black.

Shuddering, Cassy bent down to turn the mask over. As soon as her fingers touched it, she knew that something was wrong, but she didn't realize what it was until she had flicked it over. Then she saw the raw, untidy patch of pink on the underside.

She and Robert had covered the yellow roll of explosive with neat strips of papier mâché, formed into a smooth ridge inside the mask, at the back of the neck. She was expecting to see that ridge, painted grey like the rest.

But the whole thing was altered. The papier mâché top had been cut away and the ridge inside the mask was covered with short pieces of bright pink Elastoplast. They were taped untidily, criss-cross, several layers deep, so that they hid whatever was underneath. Cassy stared at them and for a moment her mind refused to make any sense of what she was seeing.

Before she could gather her wits, Lyall spoke from behind her.

'Come on then. Let's see what you've got there.'

He knelt down beside her and took the mask, perfectly calm and practical. Goldie hovered in the doorway, just too far away to see properly, but Robert came up to look over Lyall's shoulder.

The moment he saw the Elastoplast, he caught his breath and glanced at Cassy. But he didn't say anything and neither did she. The two of them watched, utterly still, as Lyall peeled the sticking-plaster away.

Underneath the first three pieces, there was just more sticking plaster. But as Lyall lifted the fourth piece a tiny triangle of yellow gleamed, suddenly bright, between the strips of pink. Cassy caught her breath. *Still there.* She didn't know whether she was relieved or frightened.

Lyall pulled away a couple more pieces of Elastoplast and then he relaxed suddenly and grinned over his shoulder at Robert.

'Well, I must say I thought you had more sense. That's not plastic explosive, pinhead. You must have had a deprived childhood if you didn't recognize it.'

'What?'

Robert squatted down beside him and touched the yellow patch. Cassy heard him draw his breath in sharply as he felt it. Bending his head, he sniffed at his fingers and then turned to face her.

'It's Plasticine, Cassy.'

'Plasticine?'

'Feel for yourself.'

Cassy reached out a finger and prodded. He was right. There was no doubt about it. It was Plasticine. Her heart gave a thud. Perhaps it wasn't true after all!

Only . . .

Only it hadn't been Plasticine before. It had been brighter yellow. She was sure of that. And although this stuff gave stiffly under her fingers, it didn't have the same, slightly oily texture.

'You must be cracking up,' Lyall said lightly. 'What's up, Cassy? Worried about the show?'

'Of course not!' He couldn't explain it away like that. 'I'm worried about the explosive. It *was* there.'

Lyall shrugged, nodded towards the Plasticine and said nothing.

'Well, what about the note on the van then?' Cassy said stubbornly. 'If there wasn't any explosive, what's *that* about?'

Lyall looked steadily at her. 'Suppose you tell me.'

She didn't understand what he meant at first. Not until she saw him glance sideways at Robert, raising an eyebrow. Then she turned icy-cold.

'It wasn't me,' she said stiffly. 'I didn't write it. Why should I?'

He smiled, as though he understood her better than she understood herself. Then he stood up. 'Let's talk about that later, shall we? Right now, we've got to get that mask mended. Don't forget, we'll have to leave in an hour.'

'I can fix it,' Goldie said brightly, from the doorway.

They had all forgotten she was there. Lyall turned round to answer her with relief and amusement. 'You can?'

'Of course. I've got some Elastoplast in my bag. I'll do it now. Come on.'

Picking up the mask, Lyall followed her out of the room. Cassy looked at Robert and clenched her fists.

'We can't go! How can we zoom off to Berkshire? Nan's in danger!'

'But Cassy—'

'I suppose *you* think I'm lying too! Go on, say it. Say I wrote that note myself. Pretend you never saw the real explosive!'

'I'm not pretending anything,' Robert said patiently. 'I'm just trying to talk sense. All we've got is a piece of yellow Plasticine and a letter about Red Riding Hood. The police aren't going to take any notice of that.'

'Oh great! So we give up, do we?' Cassy was almost yelling now. 'Let's *pretend* we don't believe this letter! Let's *pretend* it's all nonsense about dying tomorrow!'

Robert took a deep breath. 'Look. Once the show's over—'

'The show?' Cassy glared. 'What does that matter? How can you even mention it?'

'Because I'm not being hysterical.' Robert gripped her shoulders and gave them a little shake. 'Why don't you *listen*, Cassy. I'm talking sense.'

Cassy stopped shouting and looked sulkily at him. 'You're just saying we've got to forget about Nan.'

'No I'm not. I'm saying that we won't help her by racing off to the police without any evidence. We need to make a proper plan. We need Lyall to help us.'

'So?'

'So we've got to wait.' Robert sighed. 'I know it's hard. But Lyall's only thinking about the show now. He can't help it. He doesn't want to know about anything else.'

'But—'

'*Listen!* It'll all be over by four o'clock. And if you're *there*— if we're both there—I *know* we can get him to believe us.'

Cassy was still looking stubborn, but she couldn't think of a better idea. Very slowly and reluctantly, she nodded. 'But if you try to put it off again—'

'I won't. I promise.' Robert let her go and patted her arm. 'Come on. Let's get some breakfast. It's going to be a tough day.'

Cassy couldn't see how she was going to eat anything, but she let him lead her out of the room, along the landing and past the half-open door of the mirror room.

'Breakfast?' Robert said.

Lyall nodded and Goldie looked up from the mask with a piece of Elastoplast in one hand. Behind them, propped against the wall, was the big, framed photograph that Goldie had begged. The little boy stared across the room with unflinching, determined eyes. Cassy had to clench her fists to stop herself screaming.

Didn't any of them care about Nan?

CHAPTER 16

Only twenty-two hours left . . . and there she was, sitting in the back of the van and speeding further and further away from Nan.

Cassy stared through the windows at the bridges and the lorries and the blue and white motorway signs, trying to ignore Goldie's chatter from the front seat. If only she could switch off her brain until after the show!

Robert was facing her, wedged in between boxes full of paper, and she could feel him wanting to catch her eye. But she didn't turn her head. What was the use of talking to him? He didn't care about anything except this wretched wolf show.

Robert wriggled closer and put his mouth up to her ear. 'If you want to do something sensible,' he muttered, 'you could try and work out who's got that explosive. Who knew it was there?'

'Only you and me. *I* didn't tell anyone else. I don't know what you've done—'

Lyall swore suddenly and loudly, braked hard and then pulled into the outside lane, yelling through the window. Cassy and Robert were flung sideways against the doors, and for a moment they were both winded.

Robert got his breath back first. 'Don't be dumb!' he hissed. 'Of course I didn't tell anyone.'

'Well, *I* didn't take the wretched stuff,' muttered Cassy. 'Whatever you may think.'

'I know that,' Robert said. 'Nor did I. But who else could have done it?'

'Perhaps someone found out by accident. While it was at Earl's.'

'Maybe. We ought to go round there and ask a few questions, when we get back.'

'But we haven't got time for things like that!'

Cassy was so exasperated that she almost shouted. Lyall glanced over his shoulder at them.

'What's up with you two? No fighting in the back there.'

'It's OK,' Robert said quickly. 'No problem.'

'Well, go easy on Cassy. Remember it's her first show. And anyone can get stage fright.'

Cassy glared at the back of his head. 'I have *not* got stage fright,' she mumbled under her breath. 'And I'm *not* hysterical and I'm *not* going crazy.'

But there was no point in saying it out loud. Lyall wasn't going to listen to her. Resting her chin on her knees, she ignored them all for the rest of the journey, and tried to work out what to say to Lyall when the show was over. But she didn't get very far, because of the voice that kept thundering in her head, over and over again.

Only twenty-one hours left . . .

By the time they arrived at the school, her mind felt battered. The same facts ran round and round it, endlessly and uselessly. And still she hadn't worked out the sensible, practical thing to do.

She climbed out of the van, barely noticing where they were, and began to help the others carry in the equipment. They plunged into a blur of faces as teachers held out welcoming cups of coffee and passing children whispered, *It's the play people!*

To Cassy, it seemed more distant than a dream, but Lyall took charge of the place at once. Drawing everyone after him into the hall, he sat them down in a huge circle, arranging and organizing so fast that she barely noticed what was going on.

And then, before she had come to, they were beginning. After all their rehearsals and research, the wolf show was starting.

Lyall stood in the middle of the circle, his arms lifted in a huge, compelling gesture. The whispers died away. The wriggling stopped. For half a minute there was a total, spellbound silence. Then he let his arms fall to his sides, giving the signal to begin.

Cassy did not need to think. They had rehearsed it all so

often that it came automatically. Lifting her pig mask, she slipped it over her head at exactly the same moment as Goldie and Robert put theirs on. And once she was inside the mask, everything was different.

The audience had shrunk to the few faces she could see through her narrow eye-slits. Lyall's voice, as he introduced them and gave instructions, was muffled by layers of papier mâché. The world outside was almost as dark as the world inside her head.

As Lyall lifted his own mask to put it on, the chant began, coming at Cassy from mouths that she could not see. Like something out of her own imagination.

> *Who's afraid of the Big Bad Wolf?*
> *The Big Bad Wolf, the Big Bad Wolf . . . ?*

To begin with, it was all play-acting. Cassy built her brick house out of children. She squeaked in her Little Pig voice. She listened to Lyall telling the story of the Fenriswolf. But all the time, inside her head, she was busy with other things.

Nan and the explosive. Secret knocks and failed telephone calls. Postcards and papier mâché and policemen. Those were the things that mattered in the real world. Everything she could see and hear was flimsy and unreal.

Until the moment when Lyall stood up and thundered across the hall.

'Now DRAW! We'll bring you paper and pens, and you have five minutes to draw the Wolf!'

Suddenly they were outside what they had rehearsed. And suddenly Cassy was outside the tangle of her own thoughts. Racing round handing out paper, she had to think about what she was doing. And because she was thinking, she could not help seeing, too.

She saw the pictures. All over the hall, she saw the same images appearing, scrawled hastily, with thick black lines. Huge mouths gaped. Fangs dripped blood. Enormous, nightmare eyes gazed up at her and outstretched bodies leaped, impossibly long, from one edge of the page to the other.

Who's afraid of the Big Bad Wolf . . . ?

Her mind stopped dead, and she thought, *Wolf.* And at that instant, Robert slipped out of the hall and turned on the tape recorder.

The first howl made her shiver.

Suddenly, the whole hall was silent. Every note was clear as the other wolves' voices joined in, each seeking its own pitch. Cassy glanced down at the bundled monsters in her hands, remembering the six ecstatic wolf-faces raised to the sky.

As the last howl dwindled away, Lyall stood up. He spoke conversationally, almost softly, but his voice carried all over the hall. 'That is the end, for this morning. This afternoon, we will begin to talk about wolves.'

Seventeen and a half hours, thought Cassy, as she followed him out of the hall. And she shivered again.

They spent most of the lunch hour preparing for the second half. When the audience walked in after lunch, the hall was hung with maps and lists and a huge copy of the poisoned wolves photograph. And in front of them, in the very centre, was the television screen for the video.

Cassy had never seen it, because there was no way of playing it at the house. She sat very still, watching the clumsy, blunt-nosed wolf cubs struggle out of the underground den where they had been born. Watching the mother lick their soft, hairy stomachs. The commentary was practical and detached. The kind of thing that Robert might have written.

. . . adult wolves all respond readily to the cubs. When a cub approaches an adult who has just fed, the adult will regurgitate its own food for the cub to eat . . .

'Very sweet,' Lyall said as he switched off at the end. His voice was crisp. 'But are wolves as gentle with the rest of us? Do you know how dangerous they are?'

Who's afraid of the Big Bad Wolf . . . ? The question tugged uncomfortably at Cassy's mind as Lyall paused and looked round. She twisted her fingers together waiting for him to go on.

'There are twenty thousand wolves in North America and Canada,' he said softly. 'In isolated places where the winter is bitter and men go out hunting alone. So how many people get killed by wolves each year?'

For a moment there was a hesitation and then the hands went up and the guesses began. 'A thousand?' . . . 'Only a couple' . . . 'Five' . . . 'Ten thousand?' . . .

No one robbed Lyall of his punch line. He looked round at them all, with an ironic smile on his face and delivered it with perfect timing.

'There is no reliable record of *any* attack by a wolf on a human being in North America. Ever.'

Less than sixteen hours, thought Cassy, before she could stop herself. Then she stood up briskly and turned to the list she had to read. If she couldn't be more sensible than *that*, she was better concentrating on tapeworms.

But as she opened her mouth to begin her whispered chanting, she heard Goldie start, on the other side of Lyall.

'Traps, pits, corrals, deadfalls, the ice-box trap—'

Cassy's stomach went cold. At the back of her mind, a hooded figure prowled. A nightmare, moving into the day.

Fiercely, she started to recite the names of tapeworms.

But now there was no escaping from the image of her father. All the afternoon, as they built up an image of the wolf, he was there in her mind, matched against each new fact.

The children crawled round on all fours, using their bodies and their faces to communicate silently, like wolves. And Cassy saw, again, the dark figure that lurked by the van and scrambled over the wall at the end of the garden.

Then the audience split into groups. Farmers. Hunters. Conservationists. Arguing fiercely about the wolves that ravaged their village. Looking at detailed, gruesome photographs of sheep brought down by hungry wolves And Cassy thought of bombs and broken limbs. *All the women and babies* . . .

Be sensible! she thought fiercely. What was it Nan said? *No point in wallowing in the mud when you should be scrambling out.* She had to stop wittering around and plan.

But she couldn't. Each time she tried, the picture of the wolf swept back into her head, shifting and changing and growing more complicated. Dangerous, cunning, vulnerable. And all the time, behind everything else, her mental clock kept ticking away.

Fifteen and a half hours left . . .

Fifteen hours left . . .

There were only fourteen and a half hours left when Lyall called them together again. As they sat down, he stood up and smiled round the hall.

'Now, draw again. Take a piece of paper and draw me a wolf.'

Cassy raced round with the paper again, handing it out and then gathering the pictures to pin up on the display boards.

And these pictures were very different from the first set.

Some of the wolves were in classic dominant posture; head up, ears erect, tail held high. But there were dozens of other poses. There were mother wolves, curled with their cubs. Submissive, shrinking wolves, with slit eyes, flattened ears and tails between their legs. There was even one diagrammatic wolf, with arrows pointing into it, like darts, to show where the different parasites might lurk. Each one was neatly labelled and around the edge were sketches of the traps and snares and guns that threatened from outside.

Wolves. Wolves, wolves, wolves wolves wolveswolves—her head spun with them. How did you think about anything so complicated? How did you make sensible plans about something so dangerous and important and threatened?

She could hear the audience muttering cheerfully behind her as the pictures went up. But Lyall wasn't relaxed. He sat, tensely, on the edge of the stage, waiting until the display boards were full. Then he stood, suddenly, and lifted his arms.

'Wolves!'

A spontaneous cheer went up from the whole room. But he didn't smile. Instead, he tilted his head and raised one eyebrow as he looked at the pictures.

'But if those are wolves—what are these?'

No! Cassy thought. She had forgotten this final twist, because they had never rehearsed it. *No! I don't want to see those again!*

But she could not stop it happening. In came Goldie and

Robert, carrying a huge roll of paper. Silently they uncurled it and a murmur ran round the hall.

Stuck on to the paper were the drawings that the children had made in the morning. Row upon row of gaping mouths, murderous fangs and terrible glaring eyes.

'These aren't wolves,' Lyall said. And the murmur round the room agreed with him. But he hadn't finished. 'So what were you thinking of? Why have you all drawn the same hairy muzzle? The same huge eyes? Look at the blood dripping from the teeth. Here. And here and here and here. It's no accident that they're all the same. But what *are* they?'

Cassy turned her eyes away from the pictures. *They're nothing. Nothing!*

Lyall waited ten seconds. Then, very softly, he said, 'They're not wolves that you've drawn, but they're real all right. As real as a nightmare. And what is the nightmare?'

Nightmares can't be real! Cassy thought, desperately, filling her mind with the words. But she couldn't think loud enough to drown out Lyall's voice.

'What are they?'

The audience hesitated for a second, as people whispered and looked at each other. And then the answer came, in a huge shout.

'WEREWOLVES!'

No! No! thought Cassy. *Why bring them into it! They're not true!*

And then someone screamed.

Not a fake scream. Not play-acting. It was a real scream, from a terrified, tortured throat and it came at Cassy like a fireball.

Nothing is too bad to be true! You can't shut out the night! The world is full of bombs and blood and murder and death and violence—

She couldn't shut it out any longer. Couldn't fight off her terror by pretending to be practical and calm and realistic. The darkness inside her head was real, swelling larger and larger, choking her as it blotted out her small, comfortable world.

It was her own voice screaming.

Even though her mouth was jammed shut, even though no sound came from between her lips, the scream went on and on and Cassy knew that she was listening to herself. She couldn't speak, couldn't think, couldn't breathe. The wilderness came up round her, savage and animal. The ancient forest closed in on her—

Danger—

* * *

. . . and the thing leaped out of the shadows—mouth open vast, black, slavering—its red eyes glaring and its hot, foul breath strong on her face—huge and grey, with the wolf legs kicking free of the human clothing—all animal, all beast—and no time to think of Nan or what to do or how to avoid the stained, curving, murderous teeth and the blackness that came rushing, rushing, rushing, no time, no time and no defence and nothing to do except scream and sceam and screamandscreamandSCREAM—

CHAPTER 17

. . . AND*SCREAMANDSCREAM* . . .

It was all together now, Nan and the wolf and the danger and the darkness—swirling her up and away like a tornado—beating at her face and her eyes and her brain. The ravening werewolf faces snapped and growled and leapt at her and the recorded scream mixed with the real, raw scream that came, at last, from her open mouth.

Only this time she knew what she was screaming about. Not a story, not a dream, not a trick with a papier mâché mask. This time she was screaming for real danger, there in the world where she was. In the flat, behind the back room door. Inside the skin of her father—with its fangs at her grandmother's neck.

It was happening. It was true. It was *real*—but all she could do was gasp and gulp and scream and scream again, fighting for breath.

And then Lyall put his arms round her and picked her up. Quite quickly, without any fuss, he lifted her off her feet and carried her out of the hall, out of the building and away from everyone, rigid and screaming as she was.

He didn't make any attempt to talk to her. He simply walked, with regular strides, across the car park to the Moongazer van.

At first she was sobbing and catching her breath and sobbing again, exhausted and terrified and appalled. But gradually the rhythm of his strides began to calm her down and she let her face flop against his shoulder. It was warm and damp with sweat, but the warmth was curiously comforting.

By the time they got to the van, she was quiet. Lyall flicked the back doors open and put her down gently, so that she lay with her face against the ragged old carpet on the floor. Then he stepped back.

'I'm sorry,' he said. 'It was bloody stupid, playing that trick with the tape-recording. I should have warned you.'

'Not your fault,' Cassy said, with all the breath she could manage. 'I'm not usually like that.'

'Everyone's like that. Given the wrong treatment. Especially when—' He hesitated for a moment, watching her. 'Especially when they're finding things a bit hard.'

Cassy sat up sharply.

'It's OK.' Lyall put a soothing hand on her shoulder. 'I understand. It's not easy for you, being dumped on us. People often do weird things when they're under stress.'

'You think I'm crazy.' Cassy looked him straight in the eye. 'You think I made all that up—about the plastic explosive. But I didn't. It's true.'

'OK, don't flip.' Lyall put a heavy, warm hand on her shoulder. 'Just sit there and have a rest.'

'But I didn't—'

'Cassy—' He looked down at her, smiling and shaking his head.

And suddenly everything became very simple and easy. Sitting there, exhausted from her scream, Cassy felt the terror fall away from her. She realized, for the first time, what a gentle, kind man he was, underneath all the wildness and the enormous, leaping gestures.

And she realized, at the same instant, that he was never going to believe her. Not if she argued all day. She would simply be wasting her time, and she had no time to spare. Under fourteen hours left.

But there was a cool, empty space in the middle of her mind. She leaned back against the side of the van, grinning.

'OK, I'll think it over. Hadn't you better go and finish off the show? I'm sorry I spoilt it.'

Lyall laughed. 'Don't underestimate Robert. He's bound to have a plan to cover it. He probably made them think you were the grand finale.'

He loped off and Cassy sat up straight again, staring out at the playground. The terror had gone now, and her mind was perfectly clear and alert.

She had wasted too much time trying to make a sensible plan. Racking her brains to think of a way to save Nan, without putting anyone else in danger. They were past all that. There was no sensible, safe way out. No woodcutter was going to leap in, to rescue them from the wolf.

They were in the land of nightmares, where reason had no place. But nightmares had their own logic, as rigid as mathematics. And, sitting there in the back of the van, she understood what was needed.

She had to make a wild, dramatic gesture.

Lyall would not listen to any arguments. But she knew, now, that he would act like lightning if he thought that she was in danger. So she had to step into the danger wilfully, on her own, and hope that that would force him to take her seriously.

She had to go to her father.

Gazing out over the football pitches, she worked out just how she was going to do it.

The hardest part was ignoring Robert. All the way home, he kept trying to catch her eye, whispering suggestions about what they should do. Cassy ignored them all, staring gloomily down at the floor as though she could not hear. She wanted Robert to be able to say that she had been very strange, all the way home.

She wanted him to be frightened for her, so that he could convince Lyall that she was in danger.

By the time they pulled up outside the house, he had given up, and that suited her perfectly. She let him gather up an armful of masks and then, as he disappeared down the alley to the open window at the back, she went up to Lyall and Goldie.

'Shall I go and get something to eat, while you clear the van?'

Lyall looked carefully at her. 'Are you sure?'

'Honest. I—' She hesitated, just for a second, so that he would remember it afterwards. 'I could do with the walk. On my own.'

'On your own?' wailed Goldie. 'But I really fancy a bit of fresh air. It's so musty in the van.'

'Tough,' said Lyall. 'Cassy needs it more than you do.' He

130

picked up the video and pushed it into her arms. 'Take that and wait for Robert to open the door.'

Goldie pouted, but she went obediently, and Lyall fished in his pocket and pulled out some money. 'There you are. Don't bother with anything special. And don't be too long. Hey?'

'OK,' Cassy said. Not looking at him. 'I'll just get my mac.'

Crawling back into the van, she found the mac and fumbled in the pocket. When Lyall was busy lifting out the tape recorder, she took out the note she had written while she sat by the football pitches. There was no need to look at it again, because she could remember every word.

> *I KNOW that Nan is in danger. There WAS plastic explosive in the wolf mask. And I DIDN'T write the note on the van. My father is in the flat, and he's got her.*
>
> *I'm going to save her myself, because none of you will believe me.*

Carefully, she tucked it behind all the boxes of paper, spread out so that they wouldn't miss seeing it when they got to the end of the unloading. That should give her just enough time to get away.

Then, with a grin at Lyall—a grin that she made as tremulous as she could— she headed up the street, towards the main road.

And the nearest Underground station.

She sat very still, watching the stations tick past, until they reached White City. Then she stood up and walked steadily out of the train, out of the station and up past the stadium.

In her pocket, her hand curled round the grooved metal shape of her doorkey. As she reached the flats and began to climb the dirty concrete steps to the third floor, her fingers ran backwards and forwards along the rough, toothed edge.

She knew that she was very frightened, because it was only sensible to be frightened. But her fingers were perfectly steady and her legs did not tremble as she walked along the balcony, towards Nan's front door.

First, she rang the bell, because she did not want to take anyone by surprise. That was not part of her plan. She stood and listened to the ringing as it echoed emptily through the flat, but no one opened the door. She did not expect that.

As slowly and noisily as possible, she slid her key into the lock.

Her heart beat very fast, but the hand that held the key slid it straight in and turned it firmly. Pushing the door open, she walked briskly in, just as if she were coming back from school. Then she shut it behind her and spoke in a low voice, aiming her words at the half-open door of the back room.

'It's Cassy. Cathleen. I'm coming in to see you.'

As she spoke, she was looking round the flat. The hall was swept and tidy, with three or four letters set in a pile on the table. Their edges were perfectly in line. Through the open kitchen door, she could see the clean washing-up stacked in the drainer, with all the plates sorted in order of size.

Her bedroom door was open, too, and for a moment she stood staring at it while her spine prickled. He had been very careful not to leave any signs of himself. There were no clothes or books. There was no hairbrush or comb. No one had smoked in the room, and Cassy knew that, if she lifted the pillow, she would not see any pyjamas.

But she could tell he had been using it.

Everything was set straight, with mathematical precision. The curtains hung in perfect folds, six on each side of the window. The rag dolls on the bed were lying parallel to each other. The fringe of the candlewick bedspread was level all the way, ten centimetres above the carpet.

Cassy imagined him lying there, with his hands behind his head, gazing up at her posters. And then getting up restlessly, to fix their curling corners. He had shifted her china ornaments, very slightly, so that they stood in three equal rows. And he had moved the chair a fraction, placing it exactly in the middle of the wall.

Instinctively he had marked out the room, as a wolf marks out its own territory. And in instinctive, primitive reaction, the hair rose at the back of Cassy's neck.

While she was still staring, a voice spoke from the back room. It was a low, hoarse voice. Like Nan's, but deeper and rougher.

'Come on then, if you're coming. Come in.'

CHAPTER 18

He was so like Nan that Cassy caught her breath as she pushed the door open.

He was sitting on the bed, facing the door, staring at her with sharp, light eyes. That wedge face, with its high cheekbones and floppy dark hair, was just the same shape as Nan's. So were the long, narrow bones of his forearms.

But the hands were different. Nan's hands would have been busy with something useful, or folded peacefully in her lap. His were fidgeting with the gun on his knees, stroking the trigger and moving up and down the dark barrel.

Cassy looked down at the thin metal tube at the end, pointing at her chest. Robert and Lyall must have found her note over half an hour ago. How long would it take them to come?

'Where's Nan?' she said.

'I ate her.' It was a cold joke, without a smile. All the time his eyes moved, backwards and forwards, watching. Watching Cassy in case she made a quick move. Watching the door in case a hundred policemen burst through it behind her. Watching the whole of the dangerous, hostile world.

Cassy kept very still. 'She is alive, isn't she?'

'Maybe.' His restless hands moved on the rifle, altering their grip. The watchful eyes flicked down Cassy's body, from head to foot, and back up again. 'Where is it, then?'

Cassy took a deep breath. 'Your explosive?'

He nodded and held out one hand. A long, bony hand, with bitten nails. 'Come on! I haven't the time to hang about. Hand it over.'

(Time. How much time would the others need? How long could she go on talking?)

'Not yet,' she said firmly, staring him straight in the eye. 'I want to see Nan first. So I know she's all right.'

'It's her you came for, then?'

There was something unexpected in his voice. Something unsettling. Cassy kept her eyes very steady.

'I want to make sure you haven't hurt her.'

His mouth twisted into a smile that had no laughter in it. 'Of course I've hurt her. Haven't I been hurting her all my life?' He stood up, keeping the gun pointed at Cassy's chest. 'Let's go then.'

'Where—?'

'The bathroom.'

He gestured sharply, with the barrel, and Cassy backed through the door and across the hall. As he followed her, he lifted his hand, without looking, and flicked the catch on the front door. Now they were locked in together.

Turning her head away, Cassy walked back across the hall and opened the bathroom door.

At first, she thought that Nan was dead after all. She was lying on her back in the bath, with her eyes closed and her neck twisted sideways. Her face was a sickening bluish grey, the mouth stretched grotesquely wide by the tights that gagged it. More tights bound her hands together and tied them to the taps above her head.

The gun barrel came from behind Cassy, prodding at Nan's shoulder. Slowly and painfully her eyes opened, not focusing on anything. As though she wasn't really there.

'Nan?' Cassy said.

That got through to her. Her head came up instantly and Cassy saw her wince as she turned to look. All the slack muscles of her face snapped tight.

'Look, Mam. She came. Just like I said she would.' He shoved Cassy forward, against the rim of the bath. 'How does it feel to be more precious than Semtex, Mam?'

Nan's eyes were bloodshot and the skin round them was bruised, but they looked at Cassy as sharply as ever. Cassy heard her struggle to breathe with long, noisy gulps that rattled in her chest.

'Come on, then.' He jerked the gun sideways, against Cassy's ribs. 'Time I was on my way. Hand it over.'

She couldn't tell him yet. Lyall and Robert would have to

convince the police. And even if the police cars raced . . .

Cassy gripped the edge of the bath. 'Aren't you going to tell me why you need it so much? Why couldn't you just get another bit?'

'Where from? Woolworths?' The gun nudged her again. 'When I'm given a job, I do it. I don't go whining back for help when I hit trouble. Or *treachery*.'

The last words were for Nan, flung at her, over Cassy's shoulder, with a terrible contempt. Cassy turned her head, so that she could look up, into his eyes. 'You think she ought to be on your side? Just because she's your mother?'

'It *is* supposed to be thicker than water. So they say.'

His face was very close to hers. She could see the separate hairs of his stubbly beard and the drops of sweat on his nose. The smell of his body was all around her, strong—and unfamiliar.

Suddenly Cassy began to be angry. 'So where does that leave *you*?'

'Where does what leave me?'

'Blood,' she said. 'Blood. You're my father. When did you ever stick by me?'

'Ah, but that's different.' His eyes flicked from her face to Nan's and back again. 'I was spoken for, before you were born. Before I ever met Goldie. The work I had to do was more important.'

The hurt of it took Cassy by surprise, like something physical. 'Like a wolf?' she snapped. 'That's what Goldie said. *Like a wolf, defending its own territory.*' She made it sound ridiculous, but he didn't rise.

'Even Goldie gets things right sometimes.'

'Not that!' Cassy said fiercely. 'Wolves fight all right. They're dangerous and tough and cunning. But they don't forget—'

'Don't forget what?' He pushed his face even closer to hers, so that their noses were almost touching. 'What are you putting on me?'

What are you putting . . . ?

The words came smacking back at her. Those words, in that voice. And they triggered a memory she didn't know she had.

She was in a high chair—two years old? two and a half?—banging a spoon into jelly. And there were two faces turning towards her as the jelly flew everywhere.

Nan's face was frowning. Her pale eyes glared, her hand reached for the spoon and her neat, white false teeth opened and shut, as she told Cassy off.

The other face, pushed right up to Cassy, was the same—and not the same. The pale eyes were laughing. The voice was laughing, too. *What are you putting on me, then?* And the hand was brushing jelly away from around the mouth. The wide open mouth—like Nan's, but with stained, irregular teeth. Real teeth.

Oh, Grandmother, what big teeth . . .

'Wolves don't forget about their children,' Cassy said.

And suddenly it wasn't anything to do with spinning out the time. Nothing to do with waiting for Robert and Lyall, or even with saving Nan. The questions were more important than all those things.

'You forgot all about me! You used to play with me when I was small. Why did it all change? Why did Nan start sending me away?'

'For God's sake, Cassy!' He grabbed her shoulder and shook it. 'Keep your voice down.'

'Is that all you can think of? You don't want to know about me, do you?'

Her voice caught suddenly in her throat and she wanted to turn away, but he was still holding on to her.

'D'you think it was easy, then?' he muttered savagely. 'There's choices to be made that twist you in two. But once you could speak, it was too risky. Once you could go off and blab that I was there—'

His fingers dug into her shoulder, but Cassy wasn't going to go quietly. 'I needed to know about you!' she shouted. 'But all you could do was push me away. You wouldn't have done that if—'

And now there was another picture in her head. Not an old memory, but a new one, from Lyall's video. A picture of the baby wolves, awkward and blunt-faced, nuzzling at the nose of the adult. Pushing their soft heads up at those jagged teeth, waiting for the jaws to part and feed them.

'You wouldn't have done that if you were a *wolf*!' she yelled, ludicrously.

There was no point in saying anything else. No need to spell it out. She could see, from his eyes, that he knew all about wolves and their cubs. The way they played with them and guarded them, and fed them with food from their own stomachs. He knew—

—and he couldn't bear it.

Cassy saw the gun barrel rise. He stepped back until he could bring it up against her chest.

'That's enough chat!' he said savagely. 'Just give me the stuff.'

She closed her eyes and clenched her fists. 'What's so important, then? What's big enough to make you tie up your own mother and shoot your child? Come on, Mick the Wolf. Tell me about it.'

Suddenly, everything was very still. Opening her eyes again, Cassy saw that his hands had stopped moving on the gun. Nan's face was sharp and motionless, as though every line had been carved from granite.

'Tell me,' Cassy said again, softly this time.

For a second, he was staring at her and she could see him searching for words. Like a creature from another species, struggling to re-explain the whole world.

But before he could say anything, someone came running along the balcony, clattering in high heels, and the doorbell rang. Instantly, the gun barrel jabbed at Cassy's chest and he scowled at her to keep silent.

The bell rang again. Then there was a pause, and Cassy held her breath, knowing what must come next, but not daring to believe it. And it did come.

Two more rings.

The hands on the gun tensed and he glanced towards the hall. While he was still wondering whether to trust the signal, the letter-box was pushed open.

'Mick! It's me. Let me in. I've brought that stuff you wanted.'

Goldie.

Cassy's head flooded with pictures, blindingly clear. Goldie in her bedroom as the bag fell over. *What's this yellow stuff,*

137

Cassy? . . . Goldie in the back garden, looking for Mick . . . Goldie standing in the doorway, while Cassy screamed at the shock of the wolf's head. *That head's so dangerous—with that stuff we put inside* . . . Goldie with the Elastoplast . . .

It was Goldie who had taken the explosive. For her precious Mick.

The voice was still calling through the letter-box. 'Hurry up! There's not much time!'

Cassy hardly dared to speak, with the gun still pointed at her chest, but she murmured very softly and gently. 'She'll have Mrs Ramage out if she goes on yelling.'

His eyes flicked round the bathroom. Then he grabbed Cassy's arm and pulled her into the hall, tugging the door shut behind them. Roughly he pushed her towards the front door.

'Let her in,' he muttered. 'But fast. And remember, I'm in the sitting room with the gun.'

That figured. That was why Nan hadn't come to the phone. With a gun pointed straight at her back, even she would have obeyed orders.

Cassy waited for him to slip out of sight, with the door ajar, and then she walked down the hall. Through the glass she could see a pale blur that was Goldie. Carefully, she pushed the handle down and opened the door.

Goldie was standing on the balcony. The instant she saw Cassy, her face lit up, with delight and relief. That didn't fit, and for a split second Cassy hesitated. Then she saw what Goldie was clutching in her hands. Something glassy, that caught the light from the flat next door and sent it dancing into the dark hall, like a shaft of sunlight in a forest clearing.

Can I have this, Cassy? Please? I haven't got any photos of Mick . . . and I always wanted us to be a real family.

The photograph. Cassy's hands went out like lightning and grabbed the big frame. For a second, she felt the extra thickness of the explosive, spread out behind the picture, and the rough edges of the Elastoplast that held the backing on.

Then she threw it, as hard as she could, over the balcony and down into the yard. Ten metres below, the glass shattered and the bright patch of yellow fell out on to the concrete.

At the same moment, Goldie grabbed her arms, pulling her down to the ground as the gun cracked behind her. The bullet tore across Cassy's shoulder, whistling between the policemen who were racing past her and round her and over her, flooding into the flat in a dark-blue stream.

Goldie sobbed as she hugged Cassy tighter and tighter. 'I thought I was going to be too late! They were all so slow! I couldn't bear it!'

Cassy let her head fall forwards, against Goldie's shoulder. Faintly, from a long way off, she could hear Mrs Ramage muttering as the police took her father away.

'They should all be behind bars! Animals, the lot of them!'

'Didn't you know Goldie had it?' Robert said. 'I thought you ran off as a way of getting it back.'

Cassy shook her head. Leaning against the railings, she stared into the wolf enclosure. 'Why should she give it up because of me?'

'Oh, come on! She is your mother, you know.'

'But she stole it for him—'

'Sure. But when she heard where you'd gone, she went berserk. Got the explosive, dragged us all off to the police and bullied them into setting up the trap. She was terrified he was going to kill you.'

Cassy watched the big, pale wolves walking round and round on the bare earth. 'I care about her too. Much more than I thought I did. Only—it's so hard to work out. Goldie and Nan and—him. What do I do?'

Robert grinned. 'You need to plan the rest of your life now? Give it a break, Cassy. When Granny Phelan gets out of hospital, she's sure to need you back. And Goldie's still Goldie. Only—'

'Only that's OK now.' Cassy nodded slowly. 'And what about—him?'

'No need to worry about that. They'll put him away for years and years, until you're grown up. You can forget all about him.'

Cassy ran her finger slowly up and down one of the railings. But she didn't say anything. She just watched the circling, vigilant wolves, padding in their barren cage.

'They'll soon be gone, too,' Robert said, following her eyes.

'No more big bad wolves to remind you. The keeper told Lyall. *They're not enough of a draw, so they're being phased out.*'

'And all we have to do is live happily ever after?' Cassy said. And she laughed.

*   *   *

'. . . and they all lived happily ever after.' Nan closed the book and leaned over the cot to give Cassy a brisk kiss.

'But what happened to the wolf?' Cassy said.

'Oh, he went far, far away, dear and they never had to worry about him, ever again.'

'But didn't he *mind*?'

'That's enough!' Nan said sharply. 'You'll only give yourself bad dreams, thinking about things like that. Close your eyes and go to sleep, like a good girl.' She pulled the curtains, turned out the light and shut the door behind her as she went out.

Cassy lay with her eyes open and gazed into the darkness, making up a letter in her head. *Dear Wolf, Don't vanish into the dark forest again. I still need to know about you. Perhaps I can come and visit you, or . . . or . . .*

Slowly her eyelids drooped. She knew that she wouldn't finish the letter in this dream, but she wasn't worried.

She would write it when she woke up.